EXTRATERRESTRIAL

PAUL FABIAN

RISING
WINDS

For all inquiries, please address Rising Winds Press, 284 Hartford Ave #1052, Bellingham, MA 02019, or email business@risingwindspress.com.

Publisher's Cataloging-in-Publication
(Provided by Cassidy Cataloguing Services, Inc.)

Names: Fabian, Paul, 1999- author.
Title: Extraterrestrial / Paul Fabian.
Description: Milford, MA : Rising Winds Press, [2024]
Identifiers: ISBN: 979-8-9878031-7-2 (hardcover) | 979-8-9878031-5-8 (paperback) | 979-8-9878031-6-5 (ebook) | LCCN: 2024900908
Subjects: LCSH: Human-alien encounters--Fiction. | Alien abduction--Fiction. | Human evolution-- Forecasting--Fiction. | Future, The--Fiction. | Singularities (Artificial intelligence)--Fiction. | Friendship--Fiction. | Exobiology--Fiction. | LCGFT: Thrillers (Fiction) | BISAC: FICTION / Science Fiction / Alien Contact. | FICTION / Visionary & Metaphysical. | FICTION / Thrillers / Technological.
Classification: LCC: PS3606.A242 E98 2024 | DDC: 813/.6--dc23

Here force failed my high fantasy; but my desire and will were moved already—like a wheel revolving uniformly—by The Love that moves the sun and other stars.

— DANTE, *PARADISO XXXIII*

EXTRATERRESTRIAL

NOTES FROM THE
SCIENTIFIC RECORD

To find life beyond Earth... how do we even begin to define what a life is? From what we know, all organic life can be reduced to one code; an "immortal" gene encoded in the DNA strands of all organisms. Such organisms and their conscious free wills are just throw-away survival capsules to pass on this intangible gene code from generation after generation with complete fidelity. I am not me and you are not you. We are just an adaptable, carbon-based robotic vessel for the efficacious survival of our ancestors' code, and it was this code that continuously made the trees trees, the birds birds, and you *you* down through the ages.

But perhaps there exists life out there that isn't just this. Maybe once we find them, it won't be enough to simply call them "life forms," lying *beneath or beyond* our limited senses as they won't be obtained in our primordial intuitions of space and time. Even so, strangely, they might seem more alive and more conscious than we are as they may one day free them-selves of any need to rely on throw-away biological capsules and fully immerse themselves in the universe's fundamental code. From all of the extant scientific literature, all matter and energy seem to follow a set of immutable universal principles to such an exacting extent that it adds to this totalizing sense of them being "real," meaning that they abide by physical properties that can be measured, weighed, or sensed.

But there are twenty-five orders of magnitude beneath the level of the atom, meaning that, even beyond the soup of subatomic particles, all of space-time is mostly empty. But like organic life, what drives such atoms at the fundamental level is an unquantifiable intangible: Information. A dynamic code. Data that is more verb than noun. Pure, unapplied mathematics is but the exploration of this abstract "possibility space" that is self-consistent, exact, and even aesthetic in its logic.

Ever since René Descartes showed that abstract algebraic functions can be charted on a coordinate x-y grid to represent shapes and lines, we have come to realize that the observable universe is not made up of concrete nouns, but a seemingly infinite array of abstract verbs acting upon other verbs in geometric configurations and resonances that we can only perceive to be dimensional states of matter.

Theoretical physicists refer to this aspect of String Theory as "quantum fields," which are impossibly complex tangles of invisible fabrics or planes of the universe that give every unique substance its own existence; uniquely resonating *sections* of this invisible fabric are expressed as electrons or atoms for particular elements, meaning that the resonating sections of quantum fields *are* matter itself. Whether it is solid, liquid, gas, or plasma, all that exists down to the quantum level is nothing but the constant flow of a disembodied substance; the ancient ontological question of Being, which can be more thought of as a verb than a noun: "Be-ing," or, as the existentialists put it:

"Being-in-the-World"

At this point in humanity's evolutionary timeline, however, our species is nothing more than a tick that is both blind and deaf, resorting to other spatio-temporal flows of information to survive. All of this is to say that all consciousness is originally meant to be a consciousness of *something*, and our minds are made up of the world around us. Each and every consciousness is therefore a unique instance of sensory subjectivity that is both situated in and intimately interconnected with a vastly complex constellation of ever-changing data. Gene codes braving vast seas of other codes.

There lies the basis of all reality; the root of all cosmological fact and metaphysical truth; the overlap between Being and information. A happening verb. An endless whispering. So what happens when we make first contact with a civilization for whom these questions are as ancient and outdated to them as the pre-Socratics and the Enlightenment are to us? If their Being exists beyond any world, will we see a revealed truth that our limited imaginations are not yet ready to fully comprehend, much less accept?

PART I

THE REVOLUTION

CHAPTER 1
THEM

Somewhere, in an unknown corner of the endless expanse, all the light in the universe died out. A blood-red star, a billion times larger than the Earth's sun, exploded in a blinding flare of white light. In the vacuum of space, there was no shockwave or sonic boom. There was only a deafening silence.

An incandescent cloud of red gas expanded out from where the star's core once was, and in the core's place was a small, pitch-black sphere with a distortion of light swirling around its circumference, as if the sphere were encased by a glass bubble. The sphere emitted a warped and eerie droning, like an endlessly winding moan echoing through a haunted chasm of dark nothingness.

Behold, He.

Behold, the Alpha and the Omega. Behold, the "I will Be what I will Be": An infinite darkness and silence born in the heart of a dying star... and ever since the foundation of the world, He has always been watching over us... All of us.

CHAPTER 2
LEVI

Today is the day.

It's Friday, finally. I woke up at 4:45am, and the bell for my homeroom rang at 7:45am. Considering my morning ritual of taking a shower, getting changed, eating breakfast with my brother, and driving to Newbridge Middle High takes no more than an hour, I had around two hours of free time to kill before homeroom; two hours before having to deal with stupid people, student and faculty alike. It's only gotten stupider ever since the school became "Middle High" last year, when clumsy COVID-19 social distancing protocols merged the 6th to 12th grade student bodies under one building.

My older brother Enoch kept telling me, "Levi, they're not stupid; they're just 12, and you're 17." Easy for him to say, a graduate student researcher of computational neuroscience and futurism at M.I.T.. He only has to deal with other whiz kids and geeks like himself. But hey, do you know what? Now that I think about it, maybe he's got a point. It's not like my peers are old white dudes bumbling around in the White House or Wall Street enacting half-assed, billion-dollar policies that negatively affect millions of lives. Maybe I'm still too naive to know what the world is or how it works, but at this point in my life, I don't like what I've seen so far.

I haven't liked it ever since me and my brother moved here to Newbridge, Massachusetts, all the way from our childhood home of Beit Jala in the West Bank in Palestine.

Even so, I still had my own way out of the world. I sat up in my bed and grabbed my handheld radio off of my nightstand. I pressed the push-to-talk button on the side and spoke quietly, "Hugo? Hugo, are you awake?" No response. I tried again: "Hugo, come in! Are you awake or what?"

I heard his groggy voice come through the static, "I am *now*. Why'd you have to wake up so early?"

"You got some time to get a quick match in?" I asked him.

"Is that new expansion out today?"

"Just shut up and log on!"

"But what about th—"

I turned off the handheld before Hugo could have gotten another word in. I got out of bed and turned on my PC rig on the desk opposite my bed. I had my neon keyboard and led gaming mouse at the ready, but whenever one of my brother's college friends would come over, they'd wonder why I had no monitor or speakers on my desk. I'd always respond by pointing a finger to my brother and saying, "It's because of him."

Just when they'd scoff at the idea that my older

brother could ground and revoke my gaming privileges like I was his child, I'd open the drawer beneath my PC and take out Enoch's actual baby. An invention that took him years to design, fine-tune, and perfect at M.I.T.'s Media Lab as well as the Computer Science and Artificial Intelligence Laboratory.

The Brain-Computer Interface, or BCI.

It was a set of wireless virtual reality goggles with built-in speakers. But it wasn't just goggles and speakers. Enoch can explain it better, but from what I understand, the pads lining the foam cushioning on the inside of the skull cap were neural nodes that could pick up and synchronize with the user's brain waves, making the virtual reality that the user is experiencing not only more "seeable," but also more "touchable."

They also had this neat feature of acting as a dynamic, web-based interface for the user to experience the world through its own unique spatial operating system; in the goggles' stereoscopic lens, there are these eye-tracking sensors and inertial measurement units that create a transparent-like OLED head-up display that responds to any user movements or voice commands.

Now, there is nothing in the world that can't be analyzed: What is that tree? What song is that? Can you calculate the air-speed velocity of that plane flying above me? Can you translate the foreign exchange student's speech from Korean to English in real time?

Fear not! The BCI's got you covered.

Of course, Enoch didn't just use M.I.T.'s resources so that acne-covered neckbeards would waste all their time grinding away on looter-shooters or RPGs; both the military and medical schools have taken an interest in the more practical possibilities for using them in highly immersive training simulations, not to say anything of the countless greedy corporations that want to use it for stock market simulations. The BCIs that Hugo and I were using were third-generation (BCI.3s), which would have cost $2,500 each... and he gave them to me and Hugo's family for free three years ago for Christmas.

But now... today's the day. The day that my brother would announce to the world, at the Boston Museum of Science, the newest generation of the BCI; one that he wouldn't even spoil to his own younger brother. One that I knew wouldn't be released for three more years. Though I knew those three years would feel like eternity, I still had this feeling in me. It wasn't just excitement. I can't really describe it, but the words that come to mind right now are "nostalgic ecstacy." Something going back to my childhood memories has been building up to this day.

But for now, this BCI.3 was going to have to do until the reveal tonight.

I turned on the interface and adjusted it around my face and scalp. Once I tuned out the real world, the simulated reality materialized before my eyes in a flash of white light. I was on the home screen of my PC, but I scrolled down to the video games section to load a game that Hugo and I have been no-lifing for the past couple of weeks.

With the iconic fanfare of trumpets and drums came the title: *Star Wars: Battlefront.*

CHAPTER 3
HUGO

You know, I find it so funny that, in spite of all of Levi's cynical tirades against the world's many fascist regimes and organized religions, he sure did love to spam the Galactic Empire. For what felt like two hours, he was down on the ground mowing down Rebel scum while I was dogfighting X-wings.

Keyword: *Felt* like two hours. Just before the match was finished, my mom stormed into my bedroom and yanked off my BCI.3 from over my head. She was snapping her fingers around my room and, with a chiding tone, announced to the empty room, "7:25am. Hugo's room's a mess, still not dressed, bag not packed, playing video games before school."

Shit! Twenty minutes until homeroom, and Levi was still online, meaning he didn't know either. I knew mom was going to confiscate the BCI until after I had finished my homework after school, so I simply asked her, "Look, can you at least tell Levi to get ready also?"

Mom granted my request. She spoke into the BCI,

"Mr. Abd al-Rahman, this is Ms. Landing. You and Hugo are going to be late for school. Goodbye."

Once he had gotten the message, mom then pressed the power button and tossed the goggles onto my bed before rushing out of my room. I quickly threw on the nearest clothes I could find: Beige cargo pants, white tee, and denim jacket. I then quickly glanced at my reflection in my window to comb my wispy blonde hair. After I packed my books and ruffled papers into my backpack, I grabbed my skateboard and followed the scent of bacon and eggs to the kitchen downstairs

There, I saw my 11-year-old sister Faith sitting at the dinner table, her plate empty... and a BCI.3 over her face. Along with me and Levi, Enoch was also kind enough to give Faith her own BCI.3 so she wouldn't feel left out. No doubt, she was back to playing either *Minecraft* or *Spore: Galactic Adventures*. She'd always go out of her way to pull me aside and show me what new alien dinosaur, robot, or adventure she had created.

"What is *she* doing with her BCI?" I asked. I cringed at how whiney I sounded even to myself.

Mom set down a glass of orange juice next to my plate and answered, "She's been ready for the last hour. Plus, she's been taking the bus to school... unlike *some* people I know who insist that they skate to school."

I opened my mouth to argue, but caught myself once I remembered: *Tonight's the night.* Enoch Abd al-Rahman was going to unveil the next generation of virtual reality technology at the Boston Museum of Science, and Levi somehow managed to talk him into giving us both front-row seats to the spectacle. I wanted to stay on mom's good side for today at least, so I took to quickly eating my breakfast without saying another word to her. Newbridge Middle High was just down the road from our house, so it wasn't too far away; five minute skate ride tops.

I watched her do the dishes again. The plates and cutlery clattered as she took them from the dishwasher and hurriedly stored them away in the drawers and overhead cabinets. I thought about helping, but by the way she was moving through the kitchen, I figured she might get mad at me for getting in the way. It doesn't happen often, but I sometimes feel guilty that I don't help as often as I feel I should; she seems to have to do everything herself around here, as if she always had to wait around on me and Faith.

Maybe I'm being too hard on myself, I don't know. I really don't. It's always been this way ever since my dad died during his tour in Afghanistan shortly after Faith was born. The few times mom does talk about him without getting all teary-eyed and emotional, she goes on about how he saved her life with his honor, charity, and devotion to her. I could barely remember him, but mom has a shadow box on the fireplace mantel with his military portrait, medals, and a folded American flag that flew over the State House in Boston.

For all intents and purposes, I was always the man of the house: A freeloader. Well, I mean, I wasn't a *total* bum. I did well in all my classes (high Bs, low As), never missed a homework assignment, and came home before curfew. Levi and I did have some kind of knack for math, science, and logic, but it never went beyond superficial interest in how it applied to the lores of sci-fi and fantasy worlds in video games and comic books.

That's how I met the guy freshman year; we learned that we were into the same exact movies, shows, and games before learning that many of our beliefs on the world overlapped. Some kids were athletes, others stoners, but Levi and I were more than just "bookworms"... we were otaku. Ever since our AP Lang teacher gave us selected excerpts from Ray Kurzweil's book *The Singularity is Near,* we have had this obsessive compulsion with computers and the idea of a cyberpunk utopia that would redefine our broken world.

I wonder how he's feeling about tonight.
He'd better be ready.

I finished my breakfast and quickly downed my orange juice, but just before I left the table, I saw that Faith had taken off her BCI to beam up at me. Cruel as this might sound, some days, I used the fact that my hair was sandy blonde and her hair was raven black to try to pass off the lie that she wasn't really my sister, though my peers at school could tell we were related based on our pale skin and large, blue-gray eyes. She's part of the reason why I don't take the bus to school.

It wasn't that the way she innocently dotes on my every move around Newbridge Middle High was embarrassing (which, don't get me wrong, it absolutely was), but I had a gut feeling that this made her more dependent on me, shying away from other people her own age, not making any new friends. Some days, I wanted to tell her to just go away and leave me alone, but I don't have the heart.

She's so gentle and naive to the real world... So in other words, the very last person in the world that Levi should be allowed to have any contact with. At school, I always found myself having to babysit her on her way to class or the bus, always having to pull her aside to shush her after she cheerfully calls out my name down the hall in full view of other girls and jocks.

However, I wasn't going to let this bother me today.

Tonight's the night.

After months of waiting, finally, tonight's the night.

CHAPTER 4
HUGO

The plan was to meet Levi after school at our usual hideout by the cove, an old quarry in the middle of the woods some two miles behind Newbridge Middle High that has since become a popular swimming hole for the local kids. We had three hours to kill. We planned this day months in advance, but I told Levi that I felt that there was still so much ground we still needed to cover, so we were to privately review our agenda one more time before Enoch drove us to the Boston Museum of Science.

I had to make a quick stop by my locker to fetch my skateboard, my homework assignments, and... the final piece to our plan tonight.

Once I got my stuff, I rushed through the atrium-sized lobby, hoping I wouldn't run into my sister and draw any unwanted attention to myself. As I looked around the lobby, I noticed that a huge number of students gathering in cliques and leaving the school were donning what I at first thought were full-face Halloween masks. I soon remembered, however, that

Levi and I weren't the only ones anticipating Enoch's event tonight.

I forgot to mention that almost everyone with enough money to spend on the newest iPhone could also afford some version of the BCI. Levi and I have the latest third-generation BCI, but most other kids had BCI.1s or BCI.2s; obviously more outdated and lower quality, but they did have the advantage of being customizable. Themes ranged from medieval knights to nuclear gas masks to plague doctors to Grey aliens to Bojack Horseman to Guy Fawkes to *lucha libre* to *Marvel's* Cyclops and Iron Man to *Squid Game.*

One thing Levi and I've noticed during my time in school is that everyone wants to stand out: Get the newest phone, cleanest shoes and drip, freshest cut, largest Instagram or Twitter following. No one really seems to notice how they all blend together at the end of the day, hard to tell apart from one another. I won't say that I'm above all of these trends. Actually, the opposite. I'm just as much licking my chops for Enoch's new BCI tonight as everyone else; I just want to be careful that I don't lose myself to this mindset of constantly wanting to be different from everyone else.

Of course, Levi denies that he isn't any better. While we are both on the same page that the BCI is the greatest invention since the discovery of nuclear energy, he's of the belief that humanity—being the political and cultural zombies that they are—will somehow manage to find a way to fuck that up too. A constant cycle of repetition will one day lead to someone somewhere wanting something new for himself, leading to more conflict and even more mind-less repetition.

With all these masks, I had no way of knowing whether or not my peers were staring at me, wondering why I—as a notorious stan for the technological singularity—*didn't* bring my BCI to school. It certainly felt that way. Anxious that someone might start following where I was going, I left the building and immediately threw down my skateboard to circle around the school towards the woods.

When I came to the cove, I picked up my skateboard and proceeded on foot towards the 50-foot rocky ledge of the half-mile round swimming hole. The lush tree-line spanned the entire circumference of the cove, so there were plenty of opportunities for daring swim-mers to swing off of ropes and cannonball into the water.

However, Levi and I had our own private little corner of the cove that no one's discovered yet. After I was done taking in this scenic view, I walked off towards a mountain scrawled with colorful hipster graffiti and blanketed under a layer of maple seeds and slippery pine straw mulch. Under the mountain was a shallow alcove where Levi would typically leave his bike and I my skateboard. I saw that Levi got here before I did.

After I set down my skateboard against the wall and covered it under some branches and leaves, I made my way to the first terrace of the mountain. It isn't a hard climb at all; you just have to be careful where you put your foot and make sure you don't slip or lose your grip. Once I eventually reached the summit, I saw the hideout that Levi and I built around two years back. It wasn't much to look at. In the middle of a small clearing of mulch and grit was a favela-type shanty shack, only twice as tall as your typical playhouse with a blue tarpaulin roof, held up by makeshift walls of plywood, cardboard, and corrugated tin.

I saw the wood pallet door of the hideout open, and out stepped the brother of the man of the hour: Levi Abd al-Rahman. He was wearing his usual clothes: Black turtleneck with skinny jeans and white basketball shoes. I don't know what it is with his attitude; with his large S-shaped eyebrows and flaring, intimidatingly cynical "Kubrick Stare," he always went around the school seemingly ready to punch someone out at even the slightest hint of provocation.

He approached me with his hands open and greeted me with, "Where the hell you been?"

I brushed past his shoulder towards the shack, shooting him a perplexed glance. "It's only been 15 minutes!"

"I already finished all my homework and went over the museum's layout before you even got here!"

"Yeah, well, there's been a new development," I said, setting down my bag on the plastic table by the shack's small window.

Levi followed me inside. "Development? What do you mean 'development?'"

"I mean that something's come up."

"Now's not the time to mess around, Hugo! We pored over the museum's map over and over and over again, we considered every nook and cranny, we prepared for every last possibi—"

"But we *didn't* prepare every last possibility," I cut off. I raised a hand reassuringly and told him, "Look, our plan is foolproof. Don't get me wrong. We got the screwdrivers and know which turns to take when we're crawling in those vents."

"So what's the problem then?" Levi asked.

I took out a map of the museum that I printed in the school's media center and traced my fingertip over level 1 of the museum's Blue Wing. "As we went over, security is going to shut off the escalators and funnel all the crowds to the lower level here while your brother stands at the railing above us with a large projector screen behind him at the Gordon Current Science and Technology Center. All bouncers will be too focused on the lower level; there won't even be a skeleton crew on the upper levels."

Levi snapped his fingers hurriedly. "Hugo, the problem. Let's get on with it, c'mon."

"The problem is that I found a much better, much *safer* way in," I told him. "One where no one will ever find out that we were the first people to use the newest generation of the BCI." When I saw that I got Levi's attention, I took out a strip of paper from my back pocket with a random assortment of numbers: 42-21-87.

Levi took the paper in his hand. "This is just a jumble of numbers."

I paused for a moment, relishing in my own excitement, and finally told him, "You remember my cousin

Phoebe, right? I might have mentioned her a couple times."

Levi's brow furrowed. "Only that she helped my brother's team design the new BCI.4 only to get expelled from M.I.T. for insider trading of his blueprints before trying to leak them to the press, not to mention she has plagiarized some of his papers on the—"

"Yeah yeah yeah, I get it," I said. "Point is, I was playing *Halo* and *Cyberpunk 2077* with her the other night. I mentioned that you and I were going to see the unveiling of the next generation of BCI at the Museum of Science and she told me that she helped with a rotating nanobot exhibit her freshman and sophomore years. One thing eventually led to another, then I told her—"

"Hugo, tell me you didn't..." Levi said. I could see his face starting to turn red. "How much have you told her about our—"

"Enough that she gave us that," I answered immediately, pointing at the strip in Levi's hand. "That's the password to the stairwell that leads straight up to the *Exploring A.I.* exhibit on level 1. Phoebe said that both years that she used the door, they didn't change the password."

I could see it on his face: The pieces of the new plan coming together until a spark of understanding ignited a fire of excitement in his eyes. Despite himself, a grin grew on his face, and he proceeded to give me daps. "Hugo, you son of a bitch, you're an absolute genius."

"The new BCI.4 prototype should be stored there

until the moment comes that your brother will show it to the world. We'll just slip by the lower level security with some excuse of looking for my mom or something. And even if this doesn't work, the vents on the way there will be our Plan B and we'll just have to—"

"Shhhhhhhhhhit..." Levi muttered suddenly.

When I looked up at him, I saw that he was looking over my shoulder at something. I followed his gaze to the door and, sure enough, I saw my little sister's curious eyes peering at us from around the corner. She stepped out from behind the corner. She was wearing a simple white tunic with sheepskin boots; fashion choices that weren't going to get her any new friends at school anytime soon. I shut my eyes and sighed with a full-body whirl towards her.

"Faith, what did I say about following me around?" I asked.

"You're going to sneak in to steal the new goggles?" she asked in her usual dainty cadence.

I froze up. I held my expression and kept my eyes glued on hers. I didn't know what I was going to say to her, but I wanted to be careful not to show any indication that she caught us doing anything wrong. Then, with a patient smile, I knelt on one knee, put a hand on her shoulder, and looked her in the eye.

"No, we're not stealing them, Faith," I said with a reassuring voice. "We're not even borrowing them. We just want to take a sneak peek at them, that's all. It's just that Enoch told us that he's not planning to release them for another three years, and this might be our one and only chance that we'd get to use them before then. We just want to be able to see how they work before we have to wait a long time for them to be released and..."

I could tell by the confused look in her eyes that she wasn't buying any of this. She knows too much now, and she wasn't the kind of person to lie to cover for someone, even family. But at the same time, I didn't want her to lose trust in the only person she feels she can rely on. I dropped my head, knowing full well what we have to do next; I looked back at Levi, and judging by his irritated expression, he already knew what I was going to suggest. He planted his hands on his hips and paced away from us, shaking his head at the idea.

The three of us were back at my house, standing in the kitchen as my mom eyed us dubiously like a drill sergeant. It didn't help that she was still in her dietary aide uniform and had her black hair tied back into a tight and severe bun. She had already agreed to let Enoch drive us to his event at the Boston Museum of Science, but now she had a hard time figuring out what the deal was with our new request: That Faith should tag along with us too.

"I mean, I'm not *against* it," she answered, "but what's your angle here? Why?"

I knew she didn't want to say it in front of Faith, but she knew the lengths I would go to avoid bringing my sister along on anything; she'd cramp my style or get in the way of a good time. But I knew Faith. She can't tell a lie, but she was very good at keeping secrets if it meant that she felt needed or wanted by someone.

So, Levi and I came up with a last-minute revision to the plan.

"Enoch invited her at the last minute," I told her, holding my skateboard across my waist and feigning apparent reluctance. "He remembered that he gave all *three* of us BCI.3s, so he figured it's only fair that she come along also."

Mom raised her eyebrows at Faith and asked her, "And you want to go?"

When Faith nodded with a small smile, mom reached over to brush one of Faith's parted bangs away from her forehead. Mom was chewing on this, but when her eyes came to me, I saw something shift in them. She pursed her lips and tears started in her eyes. I already knew where this was going...

"Mooooom..." I groaned. "Mom, c'mon. Look, don't get all mushy on us, please."

"I'm sorry," she said between a laugh and a sob. She then extended her arms and clutched me and Faith to her bosom. While Faith returned the hug, I just froze, unsure of how to react. When we pulled away from her, she just looked at us with a melancholy smile. She touched both our cheeks and simply whispered, "Oh, my babies..."

Though I tried not to roll my eyes at this, I saw Levi leaning back against the counter with his arms crossed. I imagined that he would've looked at us with a teasing smile or something, but no. He just stared at the floor with that same pensive scowl, seemingly indifferent to my mom's melodramatic sentimentality.

Levi then said, "Ms. Landing, we had better get

going now. My brother has to leave extra early to beat the heavy traffic to Boston."

Mom wiped away the tears from her eyes. "Right," she said, recomposing herself.

As we all left the kitchen and headed towards Levi's place, my mind raced with thoughts of the upcoming adventure. A plan that was at least six months in the making was about to be set in motion, but now, a new layer of excitement coursed through my veins.

Adjustments would have to be made with Faith now being a factor in the equation, but Levi and I knew: A secret world was awaiting discovery. A new world that Enoch, the architect himself, could not tell anyone about until he was ready to show the old world.

Not if we beat the old world to it...

CHAPTER 5
LEVI

Hugo and I have visited Bean Town a couple of times before for some class field trips to the Freedom Trail and the New England Aquarium. I remember bits and pieces of my very first time visiting the city; the one part that I *didn't* block out was after our arrival at Logan Airport, right after my older brother accepted the research grant at M.I.T. after his undergraduate career at the Technion University back in Haifa, Israel. Hugo and I never really appreciated the history and glitz of Boston; it was all a white noise we had to dredge through just to get to the next hotspot.

Hugo's little sister Faith, however, was a different story.

On the car ride over to the museum, while Hugo and I were glued to our phone screens in the back seats, Enoch let Faith sit in the passenger seat next to him. Faith didn't say a single word on our trip, but I could tell from the look on her face that she had never been to any big city before; she looked out the window with wide-eyed enthusiasm, taking in all the flash and spec-tacle of the passing faces of towering skyscrapers and historical brick buildings in the Back Bay neighbor-hood. Enoch even offered to take her to the Swan Boats at the Boston Common one of these days; the glee on her face was more than when Enoch actually gave us the BCIs for Christmas. I do wish that I could have shared in her wonder, but Hugo and I had other things to think about tonight.

Now it's been an hour since we arrived and walked through the front doors of the Boston Museum of Science. On the outside, the museum looked like a modest, three-story brick-and-mortar building along the Charles River, but once you entered through its front doors, it was an eclectic realm of virtually any scientific field of study you could possibly imagine: Geology, zoology, paleontol-ogy, astronomy, physics, chemistry, computer science, and countless others. Usually, there were families visiting from different cultures, fathers bringing their toddlers, college students bringing their dates, and so on. This was also my first time ever visiting it, and already, I could see why it was such a hot tourist attraction.

One of the first sights to greet you is a life-sized Tyrannosaurus Rex sculpture with its bulking jaw hanging open to roar as it did to its prey 65 million years ago. Another sight was the so-called "Archimedean Excogitation," which was a towering structure with a never-ending feedback loop of motion; a mesmerizing display of balls and marbles endlessly hitting one another and flowing down winding tracks to hit gongs and roll down xylophones like clockwork.

As impressed as I was with both the T-Rex and the moving structure, we weren't there to look at old fossils or toys; it was merely an appetizer for the banquet of futuristic exhibits that awaited the public. Most of these exhibits were found in the Gordon Current Science and Technology Center in the Blue Wing, where there were showcases on artificial intelligence, nanotechnology, and robotics.

I'll admit that the prospect that each exhibit presented was exciting. There were autonomous robotic dogs similar to the ones used by M.I.T. students at Boston Dynamics, using A.I. to navigate uneven surfaces to walk across. But it also went beyond robotic toys; there were examples of its more practical applications in healthcare, commerce, advertising, meteorology, even accident prevention in transportation. Nanotechnology also offered the medical promise of more effectively detecting thousands of pathogenic agents using the "GreeneChip" micro-device.

Today, however, there was absolutely no activity in the Gordon Center.

Level 1 of the museum's western Red Wing looked like a dead shopping mall, which Hugo and I anticipated given that security closed off the level to the public in preparation for Enoch's dramatic unveiling of the new BCI. What we hadn't anticipated, however, was for him to use our VIP clearance to get us a quick bite at the museum's sleepy café. All four of us were sitting by the window, and Faith still had that same look of innocent wonder on her face as she looked out across the Charles River towards Boston's rising skyline.

Enoch sat next to her, across from Hugo and I. While she was taking small bites from a small burger she got from the deli, Enoch was hunched over his tray, moaning as he guzzled down his chicken fingers and fries. Honestly, I was expecting a different attire for him: Three-piece suit with a haircut. Nope. He didn't even change or shave before we left. He opted for his usual green henley shirt, gray jogger pants, and long dreadlocks. Not exactly what you'd call "presentable" for a world reveal, but this wasn't going to be a fashion show.

But I finally couldn't take his gobbling over his food. "Jeez, Enoch, at least breathe for two seconds, would you?"

My brother sat up in his chair and took a minute to gulp his food before opening his mouth to answer, "Bro, come on, why don't you cut me a break? I haven't eaten all day and I'm going to be up there for two hours at least!"

"Yeah, well I don't need you choking here before you get a chance to choke up there," I said, pointing down the hall towards the event.

Enoch gave me a tickled smile. The jab of course rolled off his back, but when he turned his eyes to Hugo next to me, he shot him a confused smirk. Hugo was glued to his phone, zooming in on an online map of the museum. No matter how many times we went over Plan B over the past couple of months, he still seemed scared of being the one to mess everything up. It's an understandable feeling, but one that might turn out to be some kind of self-fulfilling prophecy. *Now* was not the time to have any doubts.

Then I saw Enoch's hand flash out and snatch the phone from Hugo's hand. The movement was too sudden, I barely had time to react; we both watched in horror as Enoch then looked at the screen... and started laughing. He then showed it to Faith, who gave a short giggle with him. At first, I was confused by his reaction, but when Enoch leaned forward on the table and turned the phone towards the both of us, there was a Google search image of a bunch of celebrity supermodels wearing two pieces on the beach.

I laughed too, but not with my brother. Thankfully, this was part of the plan also; in the unlikely event that someone were to wonder what we were looking at on our phones, we had a separate tab open with search results unrelated to tonight's event, but still typical for guys our age. I had screenshots of math and science problems. Hugo clearly understood the assignment; however, judging by the look on his face, he regretted going that far.

Hugo snatched his phone back from Enoch's hand. "You know, a simple 'what are you looking at?' would go a long way."

"I'm sorry," he tittered. "It's just that you two and everyone else around here are so tuned out from your surroundings. Unplug once in a while at least."

I chimed in, "Oh, that's rich coming from you, bro."

Enoch gave us another confused look. "What do you mean? You think what I'm doing makes people lose touch with reality?"

I nodded. "I think that's kind of the point, isn't it? I'm not saying it's bad. The complete opposite actually: Your BCIs do a very good job of distracting people from all their daily hardships and problems."

Enoch looked back and forth between me and Hugo, as if he just learned that we feel this way about his work. I was surprised to see that expression; I didn't think there was any other way we could look at the BCI other than as a means of escape from this world. He pushed aside his tray and leaned forward on the table with his hands clasped.

After a long pause, he said, "I was going to wait for the event to say this to the world, but I want you three to be the first to understand this, yeah?"

I shot a look at Hugo, unsure of how to react to what my brother said. Faith just looked at him with clueless eyes. All three of us then leaned in to hear what secret truth was so important that he was willing to share it with us before anyone else.

In a low voice, Enoch continued, "Remember that no matter what you do, what you think, what you say, what you are, this world is all we got. We are all rooted in it. Everything comes from dust, and to dust we shall one day return. I only created the BCI to help people connect with other people all around the world, and to help them better understand and immerse themselves in this world's elegant rules and design."

He threw up his hands in a dry pantomime of his own frustration. "Of course, all you see when you look around is exactly that: People trying to escape the world, taking it for granted, seeing nothing but happenstance sufferings and roughness... Which is exactly what tonight is going to be all about..."

Enoch watched us for a moment, smiling as all three of us looked at him with incredulous looks. So many questions screamed through my skull, but one in particular was louder than the rest: *"What was it about this new BCI that was so different and innovative from the previous three generations?"* Before I could even begin to get a word in, however, I saw a tall and overweight security guard in a black tuxedo approaching Enoch from behind and leaning in to whisper something in his ear.

"Is it time for you to go now?" Faith asked.

"No, not yet," Enoch responded, "but I have to put some stuff together before then."

I remember going over this part with Hugo. He's going to spend the next thirty minutes doing some last-minute rehearsing and skimming through his presentation slides before showtime. It's what he always did even during his time at the Technion in Haifa; no matter how much of a genius he was, he still finds a way to procrastinate to the max for final exams and research proposals.

The guard beckoned us with two fingers. "C'mon kids. Let me show you to the lower level."

At this, Enoch took a napkin to wipe his lips and stood up from the table. He then tousled Faith's hair and added with a cheesy ear-to-ear grin, "Remember to stay together at all times. Hope to see you guys out there. Wish me luck!"

CHAPTER 6
HUGO

Levi, Faith, and I were already seated in the front row VIP section when people started filing down the aisle from the back to the countless rows of folding chairs behind us. In the months leading up to this event, there was a lot of talk as to why Enoch chose to host it in the Boston Museum of Science of all places when he could have easily chosen some auditorium at M.I.T. or some other public space. Sure, he could've picked worse, but still... why here? What was tonight's theme going to be?

The area in the lower level of the museum was pretty small, and I felt increasingly cramped as more and more people came in. The room was choked with whispering and restless anticipation. All of the exhibits on the right-hand side of the museum were closed under white security shutters. Towards the very back were TV crews setting up cameras on their bipod stands. On the right-hand side were a set of escalators leading up to level 1 of the museum, though they were taped off to the rest of the public since the railing above us was going to be Enoch's platform.

I could already see the title of his "slideshow" on the projector screen: *"Remember her."* Beneath the text was the iconic photograph taken back in 1990 by the Voyager 1 space probe of the Earth as a tiny dot suspended on a sunbeam; the same photograph that inspired the astronomer Carl Sagan to write one of his greatest works, *Pale Blue Dot.* The photo was an odd choice given tonight's announcement of the next generation of virtual reality, but given what Enoch told us back at the café, maybe I was missing something else here. I looked at Levi and saw that he was wondering the exact same thing. Faith didn't have the same look on her face. She was just looking around, swinging her legs from her chair with her hands clasped over her lap.

I leaned over to Levi and whispered, "So we go when the lights begin to dim..."

"...sneak along the wall on the right..." Levi continued.

"...and towards the door to the stairs leading up to the A.I. exhibit..."

"...and if we get caught by security?"

"Then we just play dumb and simply ask him where the nearest bathroom is."

Despite his scowling eyes, I could tell that Levi couldn't help but smile. I patted him on the back, saying, "We totally got this. My brother won't ever find out."

Suddenly, Levi's frown came back as he looked over to see Faith still looking cluelessly up at the platform. "And what about your sister?"

I looked back and forth between her and Levi and shrugged my shoulders at him. "What about my sister?"

"You really think you can leave her here all by herself?" he questioned me.

I let out a sigh at this. For a brief moment, I was actually considering it. She would know too much, and she'd eventually say something to mom if the topic ever came up at dinner or a party or something. But then I weighed the alternative: Faith would tell mom we both left her alone for a long while. What would be worse if we got caught? Never being invited to another one of Enoch's events ever again, or never being able to live it down and see the light of day until I'm, like, 60? I sighed again, this time leaning over to my sister's ear.

"Faith," I began, "when the lights go out, Levi and I, we're going upstairs to take a quick peek behind the curtain."

She immediately whirled to face me. "Can I come with you and—"

I cut her off. "Do you promise us that you won't say anything to mom or Enoch or *anyone else* about what Levi and I are doing?"

"Yes, of course I promise I—"

I held her by her shoulders and looked her squarely in the eye with my pinky held out in front of her. "Do you promise?"

The smile faded from her face, and her eyes widened with newfound surprise and curiosity, as if she was scared or didn't fully understand what she had gotten herself into. Sure, this wasn't a life-or-death situation, but for all of the things I say about my little sister... she was a woman of her word. She never went back on a promise, she never told a lie, she never willed ill on anyone she didn't like... she never didn't like anyone to begin with. Without saying a word, she grabbed my pinky with hers and nodded her assent.

I looked back at Levi, who I noticed was watching me making my pact with her with an apprehensive look on his face. Before I could get a word in, however, the chattering in the crowd died down as the bright lights in the ceiling above had started to dim for the spectacle that was about to unfold.

"Hugo, Faith," Levi whispered. "It's showtime."

There was no pomp or circumstance to Enoch's entrance; Levi said he never really had that flair for the dramatic. He simply strolled onto the stage and was immediately greeted with roaring applause. I saw him looking down at his shoes, trying to contain his pleased smile at what he was about to show to the world.

He began, "Before we begin, I just wanted everyone to know that I stand on the shoulders of giants. Everything that I've accomplished wouldn't have even been possible without the lovely people over at the CompSci and A.I. Lab at M.I.T. sponsoring my research and the curators here at the Museum of Science for graciously hosting tonight's event."

I looked at the people around me. Everyone's eyes were glued on Enoch's every step, hanging onto his every word; all of them except Levi and Faith. My sister stole glances at Enoch, but after the pact she had just made with me, it looks like she wasn't about to lose her focus. After we nodded our readiness to each other, we quickly—*quietly*—gathered ourselves and crept along the wall to the right of the room, disappearing into the shadows behind the escalators.

CHAPTER 7
ENOCH

I peered out into the crowd. I couldn't see Levi, Hugo, or Faith, but I trusted that they were down there somewhere, giving me support as they had these past couple of months. I don't know why my mind wandered to them though; I guess I still couldn't believe that I was up here, looking at the world I thought I once knew... A world that was about to be changed by what I had created.

I wrung my shaking hands and composed myself, measuring out each word carefully. "Given the topic of tonight's presentation—the reason most, if not all of you showed up at all—, I bet you're all wondering what's with the title behind me." I pointed back to the photo of the pale blue dot and read the title aloud: "'Remember her.' Why? Why do we need to remember her at all? She's all we've ever seen and, if you haven't already signed up for NASA's mission to Mars, she is all we will ever see." After some scattered laughter, I belabored, "How can we forget something that is at the center of everything we have ever known?"

I took out the small remote I had in my back pocket and clicked onto the next slide, which was just a mish-mashed collage of photos taken of numerous environmental disasters plaguing our world today: Air pollution, oil spills, deforestation, plastic landfills floating through the oceans. I said, "Now I could spend all evening discussing the importance of addressing all of these problems affecting our world today with good policy and good technology, but unfortunately, that is beyond the scope of what I want to talk about today." After a pause, I continued, "But I'm showing all of this to you to demonstrate that these problems are symptoms of something fundamentally wrong with our own human nature: An idea.

"Ideas aren't just like viruses; they *are* viruses. They're not alive, but they are contagious; they change their host's neurological composition and replicate as viruses do through horizontal transmission with other people until they create an environment that makes it easier for other dangerous contagions to infect the mind. Our global pandemic: We take our world, our *home*, for granted. We go about our lives in such a way that we treat every resource we have as a standing reserve, as if we're never going to run out of trees or oil or oxygen. There will always be more of what we need. And because of that, we tend to overlook the value of human life as well."

I clicked onto the next slide, showing a timelapse of rush hour traffic in Back Bay, flashy storefront advertisements and billboards, and students and businessmen plugged into their phones while acting blind to the beggars and drug-addicts sleeping on the sidewalks around them, almost as if they don't exist at all.

"We have lost our touch not only to nature, but to the world around us. The growing tide of technological progress has brought with it all sorts of spiritual implications and ethical obligations that we haven't fully tackled with. We have a responsibility to our world, but time and time again, we keep losing ourselves. And in so doing, we have so alienated ourselves to constant, never-ending stimulation and status pursuits, and we have lost an essential component of what it means to be a human being."

I fell back a couple steps with my hands up in a gesture of mock surrender. "Again, beyond the scope of tonight. I leave all of these questions to the ethicists and sociologists. But I bring all of this up to tell you all this: I don't want *any* part of this problem. I had never intended my BCIs to be a part of this problem. Quite the opposite: I want this to be the interface by which we can better experience the sublime subtleties of the world."

I then take from my pocket something I have been working on ever since I first blueprinted the first generation of BCIs back in the Technion: A tiny, square-shaped piece of gold smaller than a grain of salt, tumbling around in a prescription bottle.

The most vital, most essential component of the next generation of BCIs: The smallest central processing unit ever created.

"And so I bring you this," I announced. "The culmination of the entire universe."

CHAPTER 8
HUGO

I followed Levi while holding my little sister's hand as we followed along the wall leading up to the stairs that led up to the A.I. exhibit where Enoch's revelation was waiting. *Heh... "Enoch's revelation."* I chuckled at the thought. It sounds mystical and prophetic. Faith and I weren't necessarily brought up to be religious, although Faith, being the gullible little girl she is, never stopped questioning why there is something rather than nothing.

I told her not to think too hard about it, but she just can't help it.

That's another reason why I want to keep her away from Levi: He has seen too much over there in his home in Palestine from the world's religions for her little mind to comprehend, and I don't need her getting all confused about what the truth is. Hopefully, though, the many distractions and possibilities that "Enoch's revelation" will offer will arrest her curious mind.

Once the three of us finally got to the door nestled

in a recess between the dinosaur and sensory technology exhibits, Levi immediately got to work on the keypad to the electronic lock. "Hugo, read from that page now."

I took it from my pocket and read aloud: "42-21-87."

After Levi pressed the corresponding numbers, the blinking red light over the handle went green; Levi pushed in and, lo and behold, we found the spiraling staircase that Phoebe mentioned the other night. We both wanted to smile, but we also knew we weren't quite there yet. I looked back at Faith to see her reaction, but to my surprise, I saw that she was looking down the hall, as if to listen on to what Enoch had to say. The sound of roaring applause was faint, but I gestured for her to follow me and Levi up the stairs.

"Home stretch, guys. Let's get a move on," Levi said, shutting the door behind us as we made our ascent to what will likely be the only glimpse of heaven we will get for the next five years.

CHAPTER 9
ENOCH

The crowd was still roaring applause at me. I knew this microchip would shatter world records, but I didn't expect that it would be greeted with so much fervor. I tried to see Levi's reaction to my announcement, but I couldn't see him down there; he's down there somewhere, smiling at what his bigger brother has accomplished... despite all the hardships we both had to endure to get to this point. With so much gratitude in my heart, I became filled with an unexpected impulse to cry. But I kept it together. After all, this wasn't even the most shocking thing I had to say tonight.

Behind me, a high-resolution kaleidoscope of countless stars and galaxies materialized from darkness: One of many iconic photographs of the cosmos taken by the James Webb Space Telescope. I then went on, "You might all be thinking that I meant what I said figuratively. Nay, ladies and gents. I meant it in the most literal way possible: This BCI.4 computational substrate is the beginning of the culmination of the entire universe. And to explain why, we'll have to venture into the realm of philosophy and astrophysics for a short while. I'm sure all of you have wondered at some point in your lives, 'Why is there so much nothing and so little something?' I think the answer lies in the question itself: 'There is something only because there is so much nothing!'"

I had prepared and memorized a script beforehand to cover only the material facts of my new invention, but judging by the puzzled expressions in the crowd, I felt the need to elaborate further on this one point. "Most of the universe is composed of dark energy, which fractionates the flow of the universe's information into distinct islands; regions where the four states of matter are highly active and concentrated into different heat-dissipative substrates: Galaxies, stars, planets, and so on. The Second Law of Statistical Thermodynamics also shows that entropy and chaos are running up, meaning that heat is constantly being pumped out of these regions. But if the universe didn't have huge vacuums of nothingness for all of the heat to be 'thrown out' as it were, which would allow for even more entropy, then localized order and complexity would be completely impossible."

I scanned the crowd again, and I could tell that they all felt that they must have been missing some part of my explanation, or that they may have misheard me and were arriving at a conclusion they felt was all wrong. But I knew that they understood me all too well. I clicked my remote, and on the screen behind me showed a time-lapse of the entire course of organic evolution: From teeming microbes to fish to reptiles to us.

"While we all learned in grade school that the universe's entropy is going up," I said, "what we're seeing now is life doing the *exact* opposite of entropy; life constantly is organizing and replicating itself. You get all these sequential convergences in our evolutionary development. From before the Cambrian Explosion emerged the mystery of abiogenesis: Prebiotic synthesis led to polymers and vesicles, then to amino acids and nucleotides, then RNA to protein structures, then to the DNA of prokaryotes and eukaryotes to the phylogenetic branching off of multicellular flora and fauna. Then to our own physiology, most notably the brain: 100 trillion synaptic connections with only 20 watts of energy circulating in a 3-pound piece of electromagnetic meat; a most complex, energy-efficient substrate that metabolizes the universe's intelligence in a unique way. All of this shows that, for some inexplicable reason, life is moving *in,* not *out.*

"Our universe is definitely programmed or—dare I say—'fine-tuned' for the proliferation of unique developments of intelligence, but it was also programmed to accelerate these intelligences towards some final endpoint. Take a look at Carl Sagan's Cosmic Calendar, for example; all the interesting stuff in history happens towards the very end of the universe's development! If you were to extrapolate the entire course of the universe's astronomical development and the evolution of all organic life on Earth across a coordinate x-y grid, the timeline looks like a super-exponential J-curve tending towards an asymptote of ultimate complexity.

"And if you were to scale that all down to just a single year where the Big Bang occurred on January 1st, our Solar System came into being during September, single-celled organisms showed up in November, the dinosaurs had their glory days between Christmas and December 30th, and the entire course of human civilization happened in the last 40 seconds to midnight on New Year's Eve! And what did we get in that very last cosmic second? The Scientific Revolution, the Industrial Revolution, and—at the *very last millisecond*—the Digital Revolution.

"Entire compendiums of encyclopedias have become digitized; the age of empires became the age of nation-states, and with even more globalization, now we're seeing the age of information and online networks. The world feels smaller as we become more interconnected; there's even debate of shifting entire economies away from fiat money and centralized banks to the blockchain technology of cryptocurrency! Intelligence is not only ordering itself, but it's also *accelerating* itself, packaging and conserving all of its codified information towards an ultimate destiny; one that is found not in the vastness of outer space where life throws away its heat, but in the depths of *inner space.*"

That's where humanity has been getting it all wrong. Our destiny doesn't lie in the stars beyond Earth, but in the atoms within it.

Inner space.

CHAPTER 10
HUGO

Levi took point, peering through the door's aperture before giving me and Faith the all-clear. Once we emerged through the doorway, the first thing I heard was Enoch's voice echoing *just* outside of the Exploring A.I. exhibit. We ducked our heads slightly down beneath a glass display housing a prototype of some robotic arm.

I told Faith to duck too, but she didn't seem to hear me. In a trance-like state, her mesmerized eyes roamed around the room, darting from one display to another; videos of self-driving cars, a robotic dog traversing rocky terrain, and, most notably, a life-sized model of NASA's Perseverance Rover on Mars. Of course she'd be interested in those examples, she's still just a dumb kid. She has yet to learn all of the political benefits that A.I. might offer to fields like healthcare, economics, and environmental conservation.

As annoying as I found her, I'll admit that her short-attention span wandering from one fascinating curiosity to the next has always been endearing to me.

I can tell that it's going to take her places.

But before she can get there, we must first get over our present situation. Levi and I scanned the room for the BCI prototype. It didn't take us too long. It was right there on an open display stand, staring us in the face. Levi and I traded glances, as if to see if the other believes it also.

The BCI.4.

It was gorgeous. It didn't look at all like the clunky BCI.3 model. These looked like onyx-sleek ski goggles, only slightly bigger than sunglasses. On the strap by the temples, there were a pair of what looked like bone-conducting headphones. But when Levi picked it up for us to take a closer look at it, I looked at Levi in utter disbelief; they weren't headphones, but rather, a new innovation on the BCI's brain sensors, using less energy to pick up on our neural activity.

We did it. We're here now. But now, one question remains:

"Who gets to wear it first?" I thought aloud.

Levi and I heard another round of applause outside; it still didn't sound like Enoch was ready to unveil it for another couple of minutes, but we'd have to be quick. Levi said Enoch usually took 40 minutes rehearsing his speech and it's already been 15 minutes. I looked back down at the BCI, turning it over as if something were already wrong with it.

"Do you think this prototype is fully charged?" I asked.

He frowned at me. "And that matters... why?"

"It matters because there might only be enough battery for one person."

"Hugo, we're not doing a full marathon, we just came to quickly get a sense of what it can do! You can go first!"

"No, I don't want to be the one to break this. Mom will hang this over our heads until we're old enough to retire!"

"And Enoch will kill me if I break it!" Levi snatched the BCI from my hands. "Okay, fine, I'll go first then."

"Hey, hey, hey, wait a second," I said, snatching it back, "why should you get to be the only one to use it today?"

Levi scoffed. "Well, what the hell do you want to do then?"

A little voice emerged behind us. "I can wear it." We looked over and saw Faith looking up at us with her hands behind her back. Levi and I traded smirks, though I was more tickled and he was more derisive.

"Do you even know how this works?" I asked her.

After she shook her head, I looked back up at Levi and saw that he extended his hand back at me, as if to offer an olive branch. I considered it for a moment, and just as I was about to place the BCI into his hand... at the last second, I withdrew and adjusted the visor over my eyes. When I tapped the sensor on the right temple...

There was no flash.

There was no sound.

Nothing.

It seemed as if I had just turned off the light switch to the exhibit. There was nothing to light my reality; a void more absolute than the vastness of space. For a moment, I believed that I might have done something wrong in wearing or turning on the BCI, and I grew increasingly uneasy at the slight possibility that this would have had lasting consequences on my neurological functions.

But that was when I saw a faint and smoldering rosy glow emerging out from the void.

CHAPTER 11
ENOCH

My audience loved me. I tried not to let it feed into my own ego, so I just pushed over their applause and continued, "If life packages up its own complexity, and technology is an evolutionary phenotype of our species, then it makes sense that it should evolve alongside us as we continue to make this journey inward. Of course, humanity will continue on with all of its Moon landings, Mars rovers, and Voyager probes; as a lifelong, die-hard *Star Wars* fan myself, it's certainly fun to think that one day, our cosmic colonizations will expand to galactic proportions.

"But the reality is that that picture is getting it 180 degrees backwards. There's in fact this much, *much* faster exponential inward expansion of technological advancement: Moore's Law and Koomey's Law. It isn't energy consumption, but energy *compression* and *efficiency* that is the driving force of progress. The number of computer transistors in an integrated circuit doubles every two years, all the while, the number of computer operations per joule of energy used also doubles every two years." I raised the repurposed prescription bottle back towards the crowd.

"Put simply, technology is doing more, better, with less. The information storage and processing capacity of our technology has been consistently doubling in complexity and energy efficiency while also getting smaller. Back in 1945, the first ever computers ever made were the size of buildings, cost millions upon millions to build, and were chock full of capacitors and relays. The ENIAC computer, for example, could only execute 5,000 instructions per second to calculate artillery firing tables. Then, the rocket that landed the Apollo 11 mission on the Moon in 1969 was guided by a computer with only 64 kilobytes of memory and a processing power of 0.043 megahertz. But then, at the turn of the 21st century, the average person's smartphone could operate at 25 billion instructions per second with one gigabyte of RAM and a computer processing unit of 1.3 gigahertz!

"Now everyone, let that sink in for a moment: The smartphone you all have in your pockets is 5 million times more powerful than the most advanced piece of military technology at the tail-end of World War II and has a hundred times more processing power than the best technology that NASA provided for the Moon landing! And I don't even have time to get into the field of quantum computing; with all the cutting-edge breakthroughs done in manipulating *space-time itself* through single-electron graphene transistors and photon entanglement, it looks more like alchemy than hard science! And mind you, ladies and gentlemen, this is all still relatively *primitive,* but we are *already* begin-ning to manipulate space and time in this way with just the tools that we already have.

"Just as our universe is fine-tuned to create condi-tions conducive for insulated pockets of localized order, our advanced computational systems become more localized and compressed. One day, even tools that rely on quantum computing will be just as ubiqui-tous as the smartphone, being much more efficient with much less space and energy. Now, imagine how long until we apply it to things like machine learning or virtual reality!" I clicked my remote again, this time showing three graphics on the design of the previous generations of BCIs. "And this is where these come in. As cool as the BCI is, it's only a messenger for some-thing far greater. The task of my invention is to harness the pinnacle of computational complexity: The human brai—"

Suddenly, I was interrupted by an ear-splitting pulse, as if a massive fist had slammed into the walls to my left, knocking me down on all fours. Sparks flared down from the ceiling unto me. The blast caused all the lights in the building to dim and flicker, and before I had time to collect my thoughts, I looked down and saw that the throng of attendees was already yelping; they scrambled over each other as they stampeded towards the exitway at the far end of the museum; three uniformed security guards were already rushing up the escalator towards me while yelling frantically into their shoulder mics about a possible terrorist attack.

My eyes were still readjusting to my surroundings,

still unable to comprehend what the hell just happened. It was when my eyes refocused on the exhibit towards my far left... that I finally saw the impossible...

Oh, no... Please... No... It can't be...

CHAPTER 12
HUGO

That rosy glow I was seeing... It looked like a red nebula expanding outwards from a supernova. With it came a low and thunderous rumble that made me feel as though I were submerged in a placid ocean. As the glow gradually became brighter, it revealed the silhouettes of dust and clouds accumulating around it; too many silhouettes for me to count.

They looked like they were a part of some kind of hive or web; I then felt a wave of nausea as I eventually realized that these nebulous patterns looked uncannily like organic tissue: Nerve fibers, tendons, ligaments, cysts, pulmonary air sacs.

For a moment, I considered one haunting possibility: *Was I somewhere inside of myself?*

I then saw something far away emerging from the darkness, entering my field of view. It looked, for all the world, like some kind of fish eye swimming over these morbid networks. However, when I looked closer, I saw that it was some kind of black orb; a small, pitch-black sphere with a swirling distortion of light around it, as if it were encased by some bubble of glass or gelatin. The sphere emitted a warped and eerie droning, like an endlessly winding, orgiastic wail echoing through a haunted chasm of dark nothingness.

I couldn't tell if the orb was growing larger or if it was coming closer, but with every moment of its approach, I heard something like a radio tinnitus and the rapid crackling of a dosimeter somewhere. There was nothing I could do... The black oblivion was going to devour me, but not before ripping apart whatever was left of my mind now. And then, I heard the impossible. The tinnitus stopped, and in the vacuum of this space, a disembodied voice echoed out from the cavernous depths of the orb's Being.

"You are not yet worthy to see past the farthest star..."

It was then that I realized... I was seeing something I wasn't supposed to. I wasn't seeing an orb because it wasn't an orb. I was seeing the truth... the violent foundation of the world itself. The longer I stared at it, the more I sensed that some occult enormity beyond what I could see had shifted and ruptured, as if some deity had been toppled from its throne. My mind had no context to put it in because there was no light or color by which to see it; it was more absolute than pitch-black darkness and silence.

It wasn't just a sphere, and I was unsure of which precise point to stare at since there were no clear frames of reference around its spiraling gravity well. While I could not tell where the surface began and where the light died out, churning and shimmering ripples blossomed out from its circumference, distorting the space about it with a swirling confluence of agonized wails from the countless ancient civilizations that fell prey to it.

At its beating heart lies at the intersection of all dimensions, across every last known and unknown universe. It was as if everything in Murphy's Law was happening all at once. The sphere made continuously present every unknown and unknowable plane of existence, every evolutionary path, every chance ever and never taken, every free choice ever and never made, every sin ever and never committed, every suffering ever and never experienced, every potential of human and alien life, every "no longer" and "not yet," across every last universe... they all overlapped and culminated in this one place: A collective hybridization of all the universes' consciousnesses.

I felt this darkness beginning to defile me, devour me... define me... I soon became so strange to myself, I felt as though I had never even existed. But at the same time, I saw pieces of myself in it; every last one of me. I saw the ghosts of each and every version of myself that died with every decision I had ever made; every path I didn't take; every impulse I shrugged off; every passing thought I had forgotten.

I felt like I was truly seeing myself for the first time.

I felt myself dissociated from my own body and felt an invisible force bearing down on me, pulling me down towards the truth; I burned in every nerve and I clawed at my scalp as I felt my mind bleed into an orgiastic kaleidoscope of misshapen geometric phenomena that seemed to contradict everything abiding by the known laws of space, time, energy, and matter. Now I can never die... because now, I realized that I have never truly lived...

Now and forever, until the end of all time, I will always be accelerating, always being in transition. All I will ever desire is that what the ghosts of the universes around me desire: A still light whose warmth we will never stop chasing and never again feel... Not a communion of souls, but a mutual cannibalism... An endless race against other beings like me to devour all the light in the universe, viciously vying against one another to fruitlessly piece together and restore whatever fragments we had left of our own displaced identities against an inevitable darkness.

The hunger...

The constant, eternal hunger... the horror...

But when at last I felt myself fall from my own existence into an eternal descent, the very last fragment I had left of the world that I thought I once knew echoed up from the depths: A meek voice crying at the top of her lungs, *"Hugo! No! Don't leave me! Please!"*

CHAPTER 13
LEVI

Hugo and Faith... I was just standing in front of them...

Everything happened so fast, I don't know what happened. I was on the ground now, lying on my side while my head was throbbing with this unending ringing in my ears. My vision was blurred, but I could still make out a couple of shapes moving ahead of me. As my sight wavered in and out of darkness, I slowly began to recognize them, and it wasn't long until I felt dread crushing down on my chest.

It was Faith huddled beside Hugo's motionless body, tugging at his shoulders to try and wake him up. His eyes... they were bloodshot and dilated, staring past Faith into nothingness. On the ground beside his limp hand, I saw the flickering light of the BCI's visor.

"Stop it now, Hugo!" Faith pleaded down to him. "This isn't funny anymore! Wake up!"

I knew Hugo was capable of taking his jokes too far sometimes, but no...

Not this far...

Not this time...

"Hugo! No! Don't leave me! Please!"

I clutched my side and rolled onto my knees, but when I tried getting on my feet, I fell on all fours again. I soon found out that I didn't have it in me to even crawl. I could only look on as the little girl cried into her older brother's neck. I didn't cry because I couldn't accept: Hugo wasn't dead. He couldn't have been.

I soon felt a pair of hands grip my shoulders. I looked up and saw that Enoch was looking me over with his frantic eyes flaring between me and the scene before us both. When he saw that I was alright, his gaze went back to Hugo's body... His eyes lingered for a long while before he tenderly let go of me and went over to him with a dazed amble. But before Enoch could reach Hugo, security guards beat him to it, ripping away a kicking and screaming little sister away from her brother as they knelt beside his body and proceeded to shine a pen light over his eyes before trying to resuscitate him with defibrillator paddles.

Enoch looked back at me over his shoulder with a shell-shocked expression; I could tell he wanted to ask me what just happened. But we saw in each other that we were equally unsure of how to react. We weren't supposed to be here... but there was a fatal design flaw in the BCI that may have caused my best friend's life.

My best friend's life.

I felt the horror set in the more I repeated those words to myself. The possibility that what happened today may have killed Hugo... and Enoch and I were both responsible. I looked over towards Faith. She was hugging one of the guards, looking past his shoulder at Hugo, still unresponsive to the other guards' resuscitation efforts.

Enoch and I may have destroyed one life today...

Me? Today, I have destroyed two...

PART II

THE REVELATION

CHAPTER 14
FAITH

Ever since my brother's candle-lit vigil three months ago, no one wanted to talk to me anymore... I have no friends now. Not even Levi. Mom told me that Enoch got into a lot of trouble with the law after what happened in the museum. I think he lost his job, and I don't know if I will ever be allowed to see him again.

I still saw Levi in the hallways at school though; whenever I saw him at his locker getting his books, I tried to smile through my sadness and wave hi at him. He didn't try to hide his sadness. He just looked at me with a scowl and walked in the opposite direction. Whenever he saw me walking to him, he just avoided me. Even when we both got called down to the school counselor, Levi didn't talk to me. He wouldn't even look at me. I think he blamed me for ruining his life.

For three months, I wandered alone, restlessly looking around for someone to recognize me, just to see that I'm still here.

Eventually, I started to give up too, and accepted

that everyone including Levi thought that I was the one who killed my brother. I didn't hate the world, but it drained me of so much energy. I closed myself off to the world while everyone else around me moved on from my brother's memory. They just kept going on with happy lives, laughing and playing while my life was stuck in loneliness.

There are days when I forget that Hugo really is gone, and I go to his locker to look for him with a smile on my face. But when I remember that he isn't coming back... I forget everything else, and the only strength I have left to do is to go to the bathroom and cry into myself. This happened today. I skipped lunch because I wasn't hungry, so I went to the bathroom stall and just sat there, trying not to think about anything.

"Please help me," I called out for someone—anyone —who could tell me that everything would be okay. *"Dad?... I'm right here..."*

It was the first time I had this feeling: I'm afraid to die, but maybe it's better if I didn't exist at all. I don't want to be here anymore. I could be with Hugo again in Heaven... and no one down here would ever know that I even left.

When I didn't have any more tears left to cry, I got out of the bathroom and walked to my science classroom. But coming towards me were three boys a lot taller than me, probably five grades above me. They were wearing hoods and jeans and white sneakers. I thought they were going to pass me, but instead, they walked right towards me. I held my backpack straps and kept my head down, knowing that it was now too late to turn around to walk away from them.

One of them pushed me down to the ground, teasing me, "Hey there, freak!"

I tried to struggle back to my feet. "Leave me alone, please."

"Or what?" he said. "What are you gonna do?"

"I'm gonna tell on you!" I whine, trying to hold back the tears in my eyes.

"Oooooh," he mocked. He stooped down and grabbed my shirt by its collar. "Go ahead and do that. See if they'll believe a murderer. This isn't the first time I've beaten up pipsqueaks like you... only this one also happens to be a murderer."

My eyes widened when he said this. The tears were coming again, and I strained more to hold them back against this bully. I looked away and shut my eyes, hoping I wouldn't have to look at what he was about to do to me.

"My dad's a cop," he continued, "and when I asked him what happens to people like you—people who murder their own family—, he said they deserve to rot in jail. That's where you're going, Faith. You're going to jail, and when I—"

It was then that I saw another boy's fist punch the bully's face.

"And you're gonna burn in hell," I heard the boy yell at the bully.

I fell back on the ground, and when I looked back up, I saw Levi sitting on top of the bully, punching and punching his face with so much anger. I haven't seen Levi that angry ever since that day. The two other bullies standing next to him punched Levi in the stomach and pulled him off of their friend.

When the bully stood back up with his lips covered in blood, he was about to join his friends in beating Levi up. I rushed the bully to push him away from Levi, but he just grabbed my shoulders and pushed me back towards the floor.

At that moment, I heard a hall monitor yelling at us down the hallway. She was running to us with a security guard next to her. The other two bullies ran away, but the guard caught Levi and the bully who attacked me at the same time. He held their shoulders near their necks, while the hall monitor knelt beside me to help me up and clean down my clothes.

"Are you hurt?" she asked me.

I just stared at the ground. I was hurt, but I shook my head because I didn't want to get Levi into any more trouble. He saved me. I looked over at him, his face bruised and cut, but even then, he had trouble looking me in the eye.

Please, Levi. Just look at me one time.

I need to see that you're okay.

CHAPTER 15
FAITH

Mom didn't know what happened at school, and when we got home, she grounded me for not telling her. I wanted to tell her, but I couldn't. I didn't want to make her cry for Hugo again by telling her that I'm still crying for him. It was already so hard to breathe at home.

Levi got suspended for the fight. That's what everyone said because no one had seen him the day after; that didn't mean much though, since he could have just been avoiding me still.

All this pain... My school counselor said it wasn't my fault, but it didn't feel that way.

I sat at the dinner table with my mom the other morning, just before I had to take the bus to school. We were both eating cereal, like we did with Hugo. We tried to live a normal life, as if nothing was different. But without him here to tease or just... be with... I wasn't just feeling coldness from the empty chair. I felt it from my mom too, who didn't look up from eating her food. That's another thing I learned: No one can stand to look at me anymore. I'm scared that, someday soon, I won't be able to look at myself anymore. I wouldn't even have a real way of knowing that I'm still here.

When I finished eating my cereal, I went upstairs to go to my room and finish the rest of my homework. I walked past Hugo's door for the millionth time, trying not to look at it because I knew that if I did, I would just cry again.

But I stopped this time.

I just stood there, seeing it out of the corner of my eye. I felt my breathing rise, but I tried to control it; it wouldn't stop rising until I finally looked straight at the door. There wasn't anything on it. It was just a door. But mom and I haven't opened it ever since Hugo closed it before we left for the museum. Ever since then, it was exactly as he left it. I was tired of this. I was tired of living with Hugo's ghost, haunting everyone I talked to and everywhere I go and everything I do.

I want to go back.

I looked over my shoulder and heard mom putting away the dishes, waiting to see if she might come upstairs before doing what I had to do. When I heard her footsteps walking away to her bedroom, I turned the knob and tiptoed into Hugo's room.

I turned on the light: Everything was exactly as I remembered it. I went further into the room, my eyes roaming around the room. I saw all of his *Star Wars* and *Transformers* action figures and spaceships scattered over his nightstand and hanging from his ceiling. He used to get so mad when he caught me playing with them. I saw all of his awards framed on the walls: From the lemon battery ribbon he won in the 4th grade science fair to second place in something called the "Continental Mathematics League."

I just stood there, letting Hugo's ghost surround me as my memories with him passed me by. All those times we sat at dinner laughing about something that happened at school; all those times mom made him take me to see the new superhero movie that came out; all those times when he stood up for me and lied for me when I couldn't do it myself.

He was the only one who ever seemed to believe in me.

I heard something outside clang; my mom must have dropped some pots. I shook my head to try to forget the memories, but as I was walking out of the room, I saw something on Hugo's desk: It was his goggles. The ones that Enoch gave to us for Christmas. Mom destroyed mine, but it doesn't look like she came into Hugo's room to destroy his. It was just lying there, cluttered as if he had left in a hurry. I soon began to realize that this was probably the last thing he ever touched before he left the house for the last time.

Even if it's just a video game, I just... needed to see everything he saw the day he died. I went over and picked it up, looked it over, and put the cap on my head and the goggles over my eyes. It had been a long while, but I still knew how they worked. But when I turned the goggles on, there was no sound and no color... It was as if I had turned off the bedroom light. I saw something glowing far away in the darkness. It looked pink or red. I started to look closer at what it was when...

In the silence somewhere... I *felt* him...

Hugo was reaching out to me...

More than eyes can see or my hands can feel, I felt his touch overwhelm me. There was no face to see, no sound to hear. It's hard to describe how I knew he was there, staring me in the face. But I knew he was here... waiting for me... There was no voice when he spoke to me. I *felt* his whispers ripple through the silence and through me. I didn't even know such a sensation existed; something beyond sight, touch, or hearing.

He told me that he missed me, and that he's been wanting to talk to me and Levi ever since that night.

"Are you Hugo's ghost?" I asked the silence.

The silence told me that he was, but at the same time, he was still alive.

"Where are you?" I asked him, feeling tears in my throat.

The silence told me not to cry. He answered that he had never left me, and that he was following me ever since the museum.

"How?" I asked him.

The silence told me that it was through the world. When he saw that I wasn't understanding, he said through the invisible particles that make up the world; through a dimension that we cannot see, but at the same time, it's the only thing that we can ever see and that we have ever seen.

Then... I felt other silences... other ghosts... so many presences drowning each other out. But I could still feel Hugo's silence, and his silence told me that, ever since our world was born, *they* have always been watching over us, and he learned many secrets from them that *they* don't want us to understand.

"*They?*" I demanded, looking around the darkness for these other ghosts. "Hugo, I don't understand! Who are these other people with you?"

Then, the silence told me... They aren't people. They aren't human.

"Are they those... robot programs you talked with Levi about?" I asked him.

He then told me that they weren't artificial intelligences; they weren't even from Earth... They came from so many different planets like ours...

He told me to trust no one and go to Levi and Enoch to tell them that these ghosts had an ancient secret to who they were. That their secret is a simple math formula.

P=NP

"P=NP?" I repeated, "What do those letters even mean? Hugo, you're not making any sense! What do you want me to—"

Then the silence was gone, and in its place, I saw my mom's angry face staring down at me. She had taken Hugo's goggles off of my face and slammed them against the wall, breaking a lot of Hugo's awards.

"Faith, who are you talking to?" she said, her quiet voice filled with so much anger. I have never seen her so angry, so sad before in my life. I didn't know what to say to her. I just sat there on the floor and bowed my head. As I waited for mom to hit me, she finally yelled at me, "Get out, Faith! Get out! And never come back into this room, do you understand me? Now go get ready for schoo—"

I couldn't take it anymore from mom's words. Before she could have finished, I ran out without looking at her, hiding my tears from her. I didn't say anything to her.

I had never felt so much loneliness, so much shame in my life. Now I think mom blamed me for everything too, and I started to believe that what I have done can never be forgiven. I wanted to run into my room to cry into my pillow, but my running slowed when I heard mom crying in Hugo's room.

I went back to peek around the corner, and I saw mom kneeling away from me over the shattered frames of Hugo's awards; next to her leg were the broken pieces of his goggles. I wanted to tell her that Hugo is still alive. But she hates me now. The only person in the world that I can trust now, I'm not sure he is still alive. And he has told me he has been speaking to aliens.

CHAPTER 16
LEVI

Enoch wasn't mad at me for getting myself suspended. I told him what happened, and I'm not even sure if he believed me. He just nodded his acceptance and went back downstairs to wallow in his own self-pity. He doesn't seem to understand that Hugo is on my conscience and my conscience only. I don't care if the BCI.4 was a lemon. It was our idea to take advantage of his generosity with his VIP access and it was our idea to go against his trust in us.

I'm the one that's going to have to live with that.

I was sitting in the darkness at the foot of my bed, staring at the handheld radio resting on my nightstand. I looked up at my clock: 7:45am. Three hours ago, I would have told Hugo to get off his ass and log into the BCI for a match or two before school. But today, of course, I had no school... and there was no one on the other end of the radio to listen. I also didn't have my BCI either. Ever since the museum, the government issued a mandatory recall on all BCI models. I couldn't stop seeing it on the news; all the congressional hearings smearing my brother's name and the groundswell of lobbyists calling for him to be put on trial for his reckless design flaws in the BCI, endangering the lives of millions of children.

I'm the one who should have been put in prison for killing Hugo.

My brother was still home, but I barely see him anymore outside of passing him on the way to the bathroom. Ever since he had lost his career and his standing with M.I.T., he spent all of his time in the cellar. I wanted to visit him in the cellar to check on what he was doing, but I didn't want to disrupt him because I knew that it wasn't like him to just ignore me whenever he was mad at me. He was explosive and moralistic when it came down to it, but now, he was beyond any disappointment in me. I can tell that something about him is colder toward me.

I got off of my bed and walked down the hallway to the kitchen, where the door to the cellar was. I slowly opened it and made my way downstairs, landing on each step with a creak. Enoch was bound to hear me coming, but I didn't hear anything. When I finally got downstairs, I saw that he had passed out over his workbench. Scrawled over the walls were torn pages of his manuscripts and blueprints, and his workbench was covered with stacks of open books and research papers, most having to do with computer programming and electrical engineering, but some on cosmology and even metaphysics.

This was the first time I've seen him down here, like this.

I could hear him snoring. I took a step towards

him, but I heard the sound of clinking at my feet. I looked down and saw a couple of glass bottles were knocked over. I looked back up at my brother, not sure if I could bear to see him any longer. It looked like if he couldn't find his answers in the pages of his research, then maybe at the bottom of a bottle.

I wanted to back away from him, but I pressed forward. He clearly wasn't okay, but I wanted to at least make sure that he wasn't dying or something. I looked closely at his face, and I was relieved to see that his eyelids were flickering as he slept. I blew out my breath, but when I patted him on the shoulder dismissively, I noticed what was under his fingers.

Most of the books on his desk were typewritten or drawn. The one Enoch had, the pages were all handwritten with feverish scribblings and annotations of possible design flaws on the BCI.4 prototype and its near-microscopic CPU. I took the journal and flipped through the pages, each with repeated themes of computational complexity and quantum time compression. Most of it was too dense for me to understand, but as I flipped through the pages, I kept seeing one odd mathematical function reappearing:

$$P = NP$$

"What does this mean, Enoch?" I whispered, looking down at him as he just kept on sleeping.

I had never seen this equation before in my life, not even during my time in Math League. I'm not a computer scientist, but I'd like to think that I am familiar with the BCI's components. I didn't care that

I couldn't understand most of it; I wanted to read the parts that I could understand. Anything that could help me understand why Hugo died and meditate on the role I played in it. I didn't know what I was going to do next, but I knew that I had to bring his journal with me.

I had to read it in complete solitude, without any distractions.

I could only think of one place.

CHAPTER 17
ENOCH

I hadn't realized it had gotten so bad. I couldn't remember what happened earlier that morning. I couldn't even remember if it was still morning. The cellar was my monastery where I would spend all of my time reading tome after tome on the genesis of the universe; now it will be my monastery where I will spend the rest of my days atoning for my sins.

Levi shouldn't have to see me like this. I wondered what he must have been going through, but I was in no position to offer him any solace... since I was the one who killed his best friend. It didn't matter that they broke into the exhibit to peek at the BCI.4; the fact of the matter is that it would have eventually killed *someone*. It was just so unfortunate that it had to be a young and beloved friend, son, and brother.

Levi was always strong... even if he could never forgive me for my sins.

Though it looked like before I could begin atoning for them, I had to drown in them first; I looked down at the floor and scattered all around me were countless empty glass bottles. I didn't remember drinking from them... Now I realized I lost my soul, then I was losing my mind. I couldn't make sense of what had come of me or what I was feeling in my heart. I could have only pieced together what few fragments were left of my mind. I looked up at the papers I had stapled to the walls to contemplate my life's work one more time.

In the months since Hugo's death, I tried to make sense of it all. I thought I had accounted for every last possibility. The BCI.4 was meant to be connected through a photorealistic and globally networked virtual reality—or metaverse—, run by the latest in photogrammetry software to allow for more procedurally generated environments. Not to mention, the latest in prompt engineering and language learning that would have made higher-end chatbots look as antiquated as the fax machine; it would've allowed for more sophisticated conversational interfaces with each user's artificial intelligences, which would have acted as a personal digital assistant to this metaverse.

Sure, there were still faults in some of the hardware, but science makes progress; I was so sure that this BCI would have meant the next step in human evolution. I knew whether it was the BCI or not, humanity would eventually achieve it eventually. At the turn of the century, we saw a growing interdependence between biology and technology. Laptops, computer tablets, virtual reality goggles, cochlear implants, bluetooth headphones, smartphones, smartwatches, smart speakers.

Right now, it's just a symbiotic relationship, but we're also seeing a gradual hybridization. Our technology is getting smaller and smaller, but it is also recombining with our biology, not only becoming more compatible with the human genome, but also more *incorporated* into it to the point where, one day, we won't be able to tell where one ends and the other begins. As novel as this idea might seem at first, this trend is actually the natural result of humanity's evolutionary history.

Even when our evolutionary ancestors used tools as primitive as sticks and stones, the tools "disappeared" out of our immediate consciousnesses as we focused on fending off predators and catching prey. When today, we use a hammer, we don't even think about the hammer in our hand; we focus on hammering the nail into the wood. With every computer keystroke, we don't think about the keyboard under our fingers; we think about the words we type on the keyboard. When we drive a car, we have a sense of where the car is in space as the only thing we're focused on is which turn to take on the road.

As we use all of these tools, our kinesthesia—our sense of body position—actually encompasses them, and they become a new way in which we subconsciously experience and even *sense* the world around us. If they haven't already, they will one day become just as much a human phenotype as our eyes, lungs, heart, and hands... possibly even more so...

This BCI.4 was meant to be the *beginning* of a new shift in this symbiotic relationship; a shift not only in our bodies, but in our minds as well. The BCI's electroencephalographic sensors, which were designed to pick up neural oscillations and "synchronize" with the cortical synapses in our brain, would actually enable the machines' software to become extensions of the users' conscious identities.

Whether we choose to "tune out" all five of our senses by immersing ourselves in virtual reality environments or stimulate the senses simultaneously through the operation of robotic arms in factories, we can "become one with" our own computers. How does this apply to the artificial intelligence and metaverse of the BCI? I achieved this by understanding yet another piece of our own evolutionary neuroscience.

Within our minds, every day, we continually contend with various fleeting mindsets or different possibilities of what we may or should not become. Each mindset represents a different chemical action potential moving across overlapping sets of neural axon networks; we view the world through many simultaneous viewpoints, we internally argue with ourselves on what we ought or ought not to do, we create coping or defense mechanisms against traumatic memories, we entertain intrusive temptations and impulses, and in rare instances, we catch ourselves feeling like we exist outside of ourselves where we find even our own free wills peculiar... and with newfound evidence of *mirror neurons,* we can even experience the observed pains and behaviors of other people as if those pains and behaviors were our own.

But if we were to introduce an artificially intelligent "mindset" into our brains—one that is, though foreign and artificial, specifically programmed to know all our metadata, medical and financial records, social media, values, and goals—, our own cognitive sense of self-identity will shift to encompass the technology as an extension of ourselves. We will "share" our own consciousness with our personal digital assistants through neuroplasticity and ephaptic coupling, and the two identities become one fully integrated biotechnological "self."

A self that, one day, might even transcend biological death.

As our technology gets more complex and efficient in energy and space, it gets denser and denser and denser. I shudder to think... after we finally become one with our own technology... as the technology becomes more compressed... as it reaches new scales of *quantum* computing... what is the ultimate limit? What frontier does it all build up towards? What happens to our own consciousness?

If there was a malfunction with the BCI... what ultimately became of Hugo's consciousness?

I remembered writing it down in my journal somewhere; something to do with computational complexity. It was on my desk somewhere, probably misplaced under all of the other papers. I rooted through the drawers and checked the ground beneath to see if I dropped it; it was nowhere to be found. I called upstairs for Levi, but there was no answer. I wiped at my teary eyes and made my way upstairs to the kitchen.

But when I got there... the entire room was flashing blue and red. I was greeted by a throng of men in black suits and jackets standing around, waiting for me with their guns resting on their holsters. At first, I thought I was still passed out downstairs, and that this was all a dream. But I looked into each of those men's glaring eyes... and I soon realized that they were all too real and all too alive. *It's over... It's all over...*

CHAPTER 18
LEVI

Boston wasn't too far from where Enoch and I lived. When we moved here from Beit Jala in Palestine, I was scared that I would have to deal with all the traffic that some of my friends said they had to deal with in Gaza. Instead, we got a quiet suburb, still lush with maple trees and conifers despite how close the city was to us. All the houses I passed on my bike ride to the school were simple, split-level buildings with simple, one-car driveways. The air was crisp and smelled of wet soil. The sun still hadn't fully dawned yet, but it wouldn't have mattered because I could tell it was going to be overcast all day today, as it always seemed to have been every day since Hugo died.

Of course, I was still suspended, but the old "Fortress of Solitude" at the cove was still there, two miles deep in the woods behind the school. I haven't been to the hideout ever since Hugo died, and I wondered how I would have reacted when I got there. I cried at the vigil and beat up a guy over it. Now what?

As this was going through my head, I turned the

corner towards Newbridge Middle High and I noticed something ahead of me: There were lights flashing red and blue parked all around the school. I braked right in the middle of a 4-way stop and looked on with curiosity and concern. Even if I squinted, the scene was so far away, I couldn't really see anyone walking around over there.

Before I could get closer for a better look, my phone in my back pocket buzzed. I took it out and the caller ID said the call was coming from Enoch. I hadn't left the house five minutes ago, and already, he's concerned about where his journal is?

"Enoch, what's up?" I answered, resting my arms on my bike handles.

"Levi!" he immediately said. "Levi, where are you?"

His breathy whisper took me aback. "I'm riding my bike."

"Have you seen my journal?"

I rested my backpack on my knee and opened it up to double verify that his journal was secure in the laptop pocket. "Yeah, I borrowed it; I was curious."

For a moment, he didn't say anything. It felt like he was disappointed to hear that, but I could tell there was something more to it. He sounded different, like he was in a rush to do something.

"Enoch, you there?"

"Yeah, I'm still here."

"Well, do you need the journal back? I can come back and—"

"There's men wearing suits at the house, Levi!" he whispered urgently. My confusion soon turned into panic, but before I could ask further, he said, "They say they're with the DoD, but they're not acting like it. I think they're with some other shadow agency. They're classifying all of my research here. My blueprints on the CPU I designed for the BCI.4, they're saying they're trying to use the design to reverse engineer something. I don't know."

"Wait, where are you right now?" I asked him.

"I'm in the bathroom upstairs. They don't know I have my phone on me."

"What do they want, Enoch?"

"I don't know, something to do with Hugo's death I think."

Enoch saying that name sent my heart racing with confused terror. "What? Hugo's death!? Why!?"

"Because they say something happened at the Landings' house this morning," he finally said. I frowned at his answer, wondering what on Earth his research had to do with a family that had every right to resent him for how that research destroyed their lives. He continued, "Now I don't know the hows or whys of it, but they said that cryptographers from both the FCC and NSA detected an unprecedented breach in their packet routing protocols for their encrypted defense networks as well as a data surge in the world's online infrastructure."

"What kind of breach?" I asked.

Enoch sighed equivocally. "I don't know. Some kind of web crawler virus that adapts and accelerates every time the cryptographers try new anti-malware protocols; it not only hacks... it hijacks and somehow *becomes* the online network. The virus spiders out into self-replicating computer worms with the power to infect even the most impenetrable encryptions. What would have taken normal computers many decades to decrypt these security softwares... this virus accomplished in *less than a second.*"

"And then what happened?"

"That's the thing: *Nothing!* It's like whoever did this did so to send some kind of message: 'I could if I wanted to.' As far as we know, no technology on Earth is capable of this. The virus' behavior made it seem like... it was *living* somehow. A creature with some kind of mind of its own."

"But why at the Landings' house?"

"Because the agents say they traced the original HTTP client ping to the Landings' IP address. When they got to their house, they found Miss Landing on the floor of Hugo's bedroom, crying over his broken BCI. They arrested her and they took her to—"

I felt my breath escape my mouth. "Wait, they *arrested* her?"

"Yeah, it didn't look good to them."

"What does she or Hugo have to do with any of this?"

"Levi, listen to me for once in your life: You have got to get out of here," he urged me. "Run as far away as you can. Find someone, anyone, I don't know. Anywhere but here. I don't see a way this ends without either of us being repatriated back to Beit Jala at best, or booked at supermax at worst."

"But what do your CPU blueprints and the Landings have to do with this-this virus?"

Enoch sighed, and he answered, "The agents said

that when the cryptographers decrypted the polarization modulation, there was a pattern of code that spelled out a word and one word only."

"What word?" I asked.

Then, after a pause, he answered: "*Faith.*"

When he said this, I felt a dread rise in my heart and my throat. The panic ate away at my thoughts, but I tried to keep my breathing under control. I looked back at the school, seeing none of the federal agents returning to their parked SUVs.

"She's not at the school," I inferred aloud.

"She's evidently not at the cemetery where Hugo is buried either; the officers said they're there too. Don't go to Saint Francis', Levi!"

"So they're still looking for her. Where is she?"

"That's what I was going to ask you."

"We haven't spoken ever since I was suspe—"

Before I could have finished, I heard a crash in the background of the phone call, and my brother screamed, "Levi, run! Get out before th—" Another crash, this time silencing Enoch. Then a scuffle. Then the click of the receiver before being hung up... not by Enoch. I slowly lowered the phone from my ear, feeling frozen in my tracks as the SUVs continued flashing red and blue over at the school.

So many thoughts screamed through my skull: *Is Enoch dead? What do they want with his journal or the Landing family or me? What was that code spike?* But above all: *Where is Faith?*

I immediately threw my phone to the ground and crushed it under my heel to make sure no one tracks me. I then zipped my bag and swung it back on my back before launching full tilt down the street to my left, wondering where I should even begin my search. I didn't see how she would have wound up in Boston. Putting myself in her shoes, if I wasn't at home and I wasn't at school, and I wasn't paying my respects to my dead brother, where else would I have gone off to?

I narrowed it down to this: Where would she go outside of home or school or the cemetery to remember him? The answer was so obvious, I'm surprised I didn't think of it sooner. I rounded the street corner ahead of me, careful to avoid any roads that led back to the school as I continued my route towards the woods.

CHAPTER 19
LEVI

When I got to the cove, a dim gray hue of light filtered through the orange and brown canopy above and reflected against the rising steam of the swimming hole below. I dropped my bike in the usual place in the alcove under the mountain where the hideout was. I didn't immediately start climbing; I backed away from the mountain to see if I could have found her first.

"Faith!?" I called up to her. "Faith, are you there!? Faith, where are you at!?"

No response.

If she wasn't here, I wasn't sure where else I would have looked. Once I hitched my backpack higher on my shoulders, I began to climb up to the hideout. When I got to the summit, I went to the clearing to find the small shack's roof looked like it had caved in after some storm or vandals got to it. Dread and panic came into my heart again, and after circling the heap once, I scanned the forest below. There was still no sign of her.

"Faith!?" I called.

I was expecting more silence, but then I heard a twig snap behind me. I swung around and saw her peeking around a tree at me with tears shining in her eyes. She stepped out and grabbed her elbow, walking towards me and unable to meet my eyes, as if she was about to confess to having done something horrible.

"I didn't go to school today," she started, a smile on her face, "because I spoke to him. He's still alive, Levi."

"Who's still alive?"

"Hugo!"

I thought I misheard her at first, but I knew that I didn't. She said exactly what I heard her say. I'm no psychologist, but clearly, this little girl was still trauma-tized, and I rationalized that she'd dreamt up seeing Hugo's ghost as some kind of coping mechanism for what actually happened this morning... whatever it was that happened. I'm not good with sympathy or any of that stuff.

I'll admit, there's this sick pleasure I get in inflicting the cold truth on people who need it: Most of the time, it was either liberals, Christians, vegans, or conspiracy theorists. I felt that same impulse build up in my chest, but for a little girl as impressionable as Faith... I didn't know if I wanted to rip the bandaid now while risking some complete mental breakdown.

Against my better judgment, I played along.

"And how did you talk to him?" I asked carefully, approaching her with slow steps.

"I went into his room, and when I put on his goggles, I could hear him."

The BCI?

I asked her, "You didn't touch any other electronics?" She shook her head at me. *So whatever the code spike was, it had something to do with Hugo's BCI?* I then asked her, "And what did... Hugo tell you?"

"He told me he spoke to aliens."

Aliens? Now it's aliens!?

I coughed out a single laugh, but suppressed it again when I saw that her smile disappeared. I crossed my arms and strolled away from her, *pretending* to consider what she just said. I asked her, "And what did the aliens say to him?"

No matter how hard I tried hiding it, I could tell Faith could hear the derision in my voice. "You think I'm lying."

"No, I didn't say that."

"You don't believe that it happened."

"Yeah, well how am I supposed to know?" I said, unable to hold it in any longer. "How and why am I supposed to believe you?"

"Because I don't believe that it happened either," she said. When she said this, I looked at her with a frown. She didn't seem to have her own story straight, but before I could ask her about it, she continued, "I don't know what I heard or saw or touched. It probably wasn't Hugo or aliens or anything. But I know what I *felt,* and it felt like I was with Hugo again. It felt more real than being here with you right now on top of this mountain. I don't know what it was, but I didn't ask for this, Levi. I don't know what to believe."

For a moment, I was taken with what she said her experience was. She wasn't mad or sad; she didn't resent my dismissive attitude; she didn't show any regret over what had happened. But she looked resigned to the world, as if she were looking for some way back into herself. I shook my head, still refusing to believe her. But that still left so many unanswered questions: Why did the government want Enoch's CPU blueprints? How did Faith's turning on Hugo's BCI of all things cause that code spike?

That was when Faith blurted, "Hugo said the aliens told him that P=NP!" Something about what she said... I heard or read about it somewhere. When I turned around to face her again, she added, "He told me to ask you and Enoch about it. But before Hugo could tell me what it meant, mom took the goggles off and broke them. She's still sad about... everything..."

The gears turned in my mind. I took off my bag and took out my brother's journal to flip through the pages to find the math function my brother wrote repeatedly. Lo and behold, there it was: P=NP. I looked back up at Faith as if she were a new discovery. I didn't know what to make of it all. But now, it was clear to me what Faith saw and what Enoch told me... It was all connected somehow.

But there was no way in hell that Hugo's spirit was somehow haunting Faith to talk to her about aliens. It must have been an illusion for something else; she thought she saw—or rather, *felt*—Hugo again, when really, the code spike scrambled the BCI's neural nodes, making her unconsciously construct an image of Hugo from her memories or something like that. How that was possible, if it was possible, I couldn't explain. It had to be anything other than aliens; anything other than what Faith was telling me.

But even if it was... why *her* specifically?

Why *Faith?*

After checking my watch, I gestured my head down the mountain. "There's some abandoned tracks that cut through these woods here; it will take us down to Fallow Park Station downtown. I got money to get us an MBTA pass there to Back Bay in Boston; I think I know someone there that might be able to help us." Faith had a dumb look on her face; either she didn't listen to or didn't understand what I just said. I didn't feel like repeating myself since the next commuter rail to Boston was going to be in about half an hour or so... assuming Homeland Security didn't reach the station yet. I started down the mountain.

"Hey, wait!" Faith called, following shortly behind me as we both climbed down carefully. When we got to the bottom, I walked the beaten path away from the cove. Faith just kept calling for me, "Levi, what do you think happened to me?"

I wasn't on the path long until I stepped out of the treeline and found the gravelly railroad tracks. I looked both ways before going left; I didn't look back at Faith. I just kept pressing on, hoping that Faith wouldn't notice that I was unsure of what our next step would be. I heard the leaves crunching behind me growing louder until she ran up next to me, looking up with the same stare she would always give me and Hugo.

"What is P and NP? Who are we looking for? How can aliens talk to Hugo? How can Hugo talk to me—"

I couldn't take it anymore. "Look, let's get a couple

of things straight now, okay?" I said, stopping her in the middle of the tracks to look her in the eye. "You don't bring up what happened back there. *Ever.* There's people looking for us both now and I don't want anything we say to catch up to us. Personally, I don't know what you saw this morning; Hugo, aliens, whatever. All I know is that it all somehow means something... and we can't risk losing it.

"And second, I want to make it very clear: We are *not friends.* Don't talk to me like we are. All I know is that Enoch needs your help, and you need mine. We can't trust or rely on anyone else, including the police; *nobody* else other than each other. Now, if anyone asks, we'll be—oh, I don't know—I'll be Hugh and you'll be Mia. Do you understand me?"

I could tell by the tear in her eye that I had struck a nerve with her. Her face fell small and downcast, and her dazed eyes swayed and flickered as if the overwhelming upset was leaving her lightheaded. Without saying anything else to me, she nodded once and walked right past me. I looked on, watching the hurt in her every step. I really took no pleasure in telling her, but I knew that it was better that she knew now before I hurt her more down the line. I knew I was bound to say something that might tear apart whatever fragile lie was keeping her together after seeing her brother die right in front of her.

I then sighed and whispered to myself, "Well, Phoebe, it shouldn't be too hard to find you."

CHAPTER 20
ENOCH

When these shady "men in black" in my house caught me talking on the phone in the bathroom, we traded blows; just when they thought they had knocked me out, I quietly ended the call before they could have gotten a trace on Levi. After they found out that I was still awake, they yanked me back up to my feet, pulled a rag over my face, and shoved me in the back of a van.

For a good two hours, I couldn't see where they were taking me. They wouldn't tell me anything, no matter how many times I demanded it. I didn't know what else they wanted with me, but it seemed that they weren't satisfied with taking everything I'd ever accomplished away from me.

Now, they want my brother.

I felt the van stop before the men dragged me out by my bound wrists. We walked into what sounded like a large atrium; I could hear our footsteps and their voices echoing off towering marble walls, and I sensed a white light filtering through the threads of the rag over my face. The men then led me around a corner before we walked down a dark concrete corridor with dimly flickering sconce lamps.

When they finally brought me to a room, they took the bag off my head. The room was lit by the flickering lights of overhead fluorescent tubes, and the walls were made of white-plastered cinder blocks; except for a long one-way mirror and a mounted camera in the ceiling corner, there was only a metal table and a bolted-down chair in the middle of the plain room.

"What do you want with my family!?" I demanded again.

One of the men responded by grabbing me by my shirt collar and forcing me down on the chair. Another one came towards the table with a manilla folder in hand and let it fall on the table. Some of the papers slid out, revealing a name and a face Levi and I had hoped we'd never see ever again.

The man came forward and told me, "How can you presume to say anything about the future if you aren't willing to face your own past?"

So many thoughts were screaming through my head, wondering what my father had to do with what they were looking for. I offered, "Just take me. I don't know what you want, and I don't know anything about my father anymore, but just leave Levi out of this, please. We want nothing to do with the conflict with the Israelis and—"

"No, we didn't bring you here for that," the man interrupted, "but we're showing you what our Blob can do if you don't comply with our demands."

"Blob?" I repeated.

"Us," the man clarified.

"Who the hell are all of you!?"

"We're a special access program of the federal government, SCI-classified above top secret."

"Well, what do you want with me!?"

"You don't have to play stupid with us, Enoch; we've tapped into your conversation with Levi before you ended the call. As you told him, something big just happened: A data surge sent seismic disruptions through JWICS, SIPRNet, and other telecom channels the likes of which not only the DoD or NSA, but the global computer grid at large had never seen before.

"That surge had an encryption signature that spelled out that girl's name, who so conveniently happens to be the sister to the sole victim of your invention. But not only that. Our cryptographers also tell us that the signature also has another code encrypted in it; a code that has the power to alter the course of history... and your brother has both keys to unlocking its power: Your journal and the girl."

I demanded one more time, "What more can I do to help? You already took everything I have; my prototypes, my blueprints, my research, my standing, everything. What more could you possibly want from me?"

"You invented the BCI," the man answered. "All of your research means nothing if we don't have the inventor to brief us each step of the way."

"And why should I help you?"

The man shrugged and paced away from the table. "Once we learn more about how far the girl will take this, you help decrypt the source of the data surge...

you and your brother will be compensated with hefty annuities established in your names subject to the condition of your silence. Would you like for your brother to attend your classes on a full ride at M.I.T.?"

I chewed on this deal, and for a moment, I wondered if I would have been selling my soul to the devil. Then a concern occurred to me: "And what'll happen to Faith?"

At that moment, the door across the room opened, and two figures stepped in. At first, I couldn't get a good look at the figures since they mostly stood in the shadows, but I immediately saw that one of them looked starkly different from the rest of the men in the room. As I looked closer, however, I began to recognize the person's face, and became filled with a horrifying realization of the unspeakable treachery that was committed against my family and Hugo's. The shadow stepped forth with a shoebox-sized box in hand and placed it carefully on the table next to me and the man.

"You?" I managed out in a fierce whisper, provoking no reaction from the shadow, who simply walked back to the corner.

When I couldn't take my eyes off of this traitor, the man in front of me snapped his finger at my eyes and finally answered my question, "That will be *their* concern, Enoch. You? You just worry about your brother. Hey, look at me. Now, we're going to need you and your old friend over there to explain every single detail of your BCI.4 to us." He then opened the box that Judas brought, and took out something impossible: Another BCI.4. The man repeated, *"Every. Single. Detail."*

PART III

THE TRUTH

CHAPTER 21
FAITH

I felt him again in my dreams. The silence was so much. I didn't have Hugo's BCI this time, but there was something about the silence that felt... different... It wasn't Hugo, but it felt so much like what he had become, whatever he was...

Only this time, I did see something.

It wasn't like anything I've ever seen before. I didn't know what it was, if you could even call it an "it." I still don't know how to describe it. It was in front of me, but it was so big and so towering, it was almost surrounding me; it felt like it was becoming my surroundings; it felt like my surroundings. It looked like a solar eclipse, but at the same time, it didn't look anything like a solar eclipse.

It was dark, but it was more than black. For some reason, I thought I was floating in space, but strangely, as I got closer to its surface, I felt like my body became heavier. I couldn't move. I could barely even breathe.

Then, the silence spoke to me, just like Hugo's silence spoke to me back in mom's house. But this wasn't just one voice I was feeling go through me; there were countless voices all screaming over each other, all coming from this ring of fire. I grabbed my head, trying to block them all out. But some of them still came through, and they told me that Levi and I were making a horrible mistake chasing after Hugo's secret.

That Hugo was dangerous... and I should stop him before it's too late.

"Stop Hugo?" I asked the silence. "Why on Earth should I stop Hugo?"

They told me that he was going to destroy the whole world as I knew it; that humans are not ready to learn or accept the discovery that they had made; the discovery that made them become what they are now.

But just before I could ask the silence why Hugo was dangerous... I was startled awake by something; the train must have hit a bump in the tracks. I looked out the window and saw tall buildings and skyscrapers against the cloudy sky; it seemed like every day since Hugo died, no matter where I went, fog and rain clouds blocked out the sun and sky.

I used to love Boston before the accident. There was always so much to see. Even on the train from Fallow Station, I think I saw almost everything there was to see of the city. I saw the harp triangles of Zakim Bridge, the square *Citigo* sign over the Big Green Monster at Fenway Park, the gateway arch and garlands of lanterns of Chinatown, Duck Tour boats with wheels driving towards the Charles River and taxis with posters for the Blue Man Group.

I then looked at the train's destination sign: Next stop is Ruggles. The train wasn't there yet, but I knew we were getting close. I looked down at my lap. Levi had tried to stay awake to "watch for anyone following us," but he didn't last ten minutes before he fell asleep on my shoulder and then my lap.

Even in his sleep, he still had that same unfriendly scowl; it was probably just the large eyebrows. I didn't want to disturb him. It wasn't even 12 o'clock, and it already felt like a very long day; we both needed sleep. But he also hurt my feelings earlier today when he told me that he didn't want to be my friend. I wanted to believe that he didn't mean it, but I wasn't sure since we were both still sad over my brother's "death."

I nudged his shoulder to try to wake him. "Hey, Levi? Levi, I think we're almost there."

Levi groaned awake, sitting upright in his seat and rubbing his eyes with one of his knuckles. He looked over my head out the window to see the passing skyline of Boston. I can tell that he wants to hide that he doesn't know where to go or what to do next, but there was an answer out there... somewhere.

I want to believe that too.

"Remember, Faith, whatever happens, just..."

"...stay close," I said. "I know."

"Good," he said, going back to looking out the window. "And remember: Your name is Mia and my name is Hugh."

It wasn't long before a voice in the intercom announced, *"Back Bay Station next. Back Bay."*

CHAPTER 22
FAITH

I saw flocks of pigeons flying up to the skyscrapers and church towers. The city is so pretty the way the houses and buildings would sparkle with so many colors in the night. There were more clothing stores, coffee shops, and bodegas on one street than there were in downtown Newbridge. I remember mom told us to look both ways in the street, since honking cars and trucks always rushed by and sometimes did not obey street signs. Mom told me to not touch anything either because there were germs everywhere on handlebars, railings, chairs; she even told me that some people went to the bathroom behind buildings!

Mom also told me "stranger danger," but I've never seen someone in Boston be mean to me yet. Some people smelled like skunk and were scary looking: Dirty clothes, parkas, long gray beards, wrinkly faces, staring eyes, trash bags and shopping carts. Most people were too distracted or in a hurry somewhere, always on their phones wearing business suits or college sweaters. Other people were very nice: People playing guitars, drums, and trumpets, vendors selling peanuts and hotdogs, construction workers carrying wood and boxes, even some men dressed like colonists and soldiers from the Revolution. There were also some people standing at street corners who gave me a pamphlet and told me that I could see my brother again in Heaven if I followed their directions; that was so exciting, but Levi didn't like them for some reason. He just told them we weren't interested.

I wondered where we were in a hurry to, then Levi pointed up the street to a long, gray brick building: The Boston Public Library. That was one of the first places we saw when we got out of the train station. We had to cross a lot of streets and push through so many crowds on our way there. When we got there, Levi wanted to go in immediately, but I just stood there a while longer to try to read all the names engraved on the building's face. I recognized a couple from school: Darwin, Galileo, Socrates, Plato, Aristotle.

On top of the first platform of the front steps were two bronze women wearing robes and sitting on thrones of stone: To the left was *Science* holding a globe, and to the right was *Art* holding a palette and brush. I marveled at these two guardians of truth and beauty for a short while before Levi grabbed my arm and almost dragged me inside through the towering bronze front doors.

When we were inside, I immediately took in the high arching ceilings and the pink marble walls. Ahead of us was a set of stairs carved out of yellow marble with some pink and black stripes in the stone. The stairs led up to a landing that was guarded by two sculptures of lions; as we passed them, Levi said they were built to honor the memory of Civil War soldiers. The stairs then split and turned ninety degrees to the right and left.

We took the left steps, and once on the second floor, I noticed some four very large, Renaissance-style murals that looked like they belonged in art museums in Europe. They were of different times in ancient Greece, with scientists, philosophers, and poets standing around gardens and columned ruins talking about the meaning of life. We then entered a big square-shaped room, where I saw a painting of robed angels bringing the Holy Grail down to a kneeling knight. I know nothing about history like Levi did, but everything I had seen in that building was so beautiful, it felt like I stepped into a completely different world; a world where the truth was artistic and beautiful. I looked back at Levi, and he didn't look at all impressed by all the artwork around him.

We took a left through one of the doors to cut through what looked like the main reading room of the library. There was the hushed rustling of papers and shuffling of books echoing off the walls and the 50-foot-high arched ceiling above. College students sat at the oak tables going up and down the room, each with four green-coned bank lamps. There were also long bookcases lining each wall. With the arched windows to the right of the room, I felt like I was walking down the aisle of a church rather than through a library.

"What are we looking for here?" I asked Levi.

"We're looking for the yellow pages," he answered.

"What are yellow pages?"

"It's basically a registry of almost every person in Boston with their contact info. I'm going to be looking up your cousin: Phoebe Landing."

I darted my eyes up at Levi with surprise and joy filling my heart. "Cousin Phoebe?"

"Yeah, she helped my brother design the BCI. She got expelled from M.I.T., but she might still know something I don't."

"I haven't seen her in forever!"

"And how long's forever to you?" he asked me.

"She was always busy with college," I answered. "I haven't seen her since I was just three."

"Yeah, you wouldn't happen to know where she lives now, do you?"

"I think I know what her building looks like, but I don't remember what street it was exactly."

Levi gave me a short nod. "Well I guess that can help us later. Just stick close to me, we're gonna go look for a librarian."

CHAPTER 23
LEVI

At the other end of the reading hall was the librarian's front desk. I was still dragging Faith by her elbow. Ever since we got off the commuter rail, her big eyes wandered to every passing curiosity or art piece. I didn't see what was so special about every little thing she saw; all I cared about was finding the truth.

When we got to the front desk, we were "greeted" by a woman who looked my brother's age. It wasn't so much a greeting as it was a disinterested glance. I'll admit, I have a habit of profiling people for their looks: This one has what some girls in my grade call a "resting bitch face" syndrome.

She had blonde hair, cold blue-gray eyes, hula-hoop earrings, long stiletto nails, and was wearing a black tee with skinny jeans. She didn't look like she wanted to be here at all; she just leaned forward over the desk, looking at her phone while chewing gum. When she noticed us standing at the other side of the desk, she looked around, as if she thought we were looking at someone else.

"Can I help you?" she asked. I could tell by the attitude that this was going to be pleasant.

I cleared my throat and asked her, "Yeah, we're looking for the yellow pages."

"What for? You looking for a video game arcade or something?"

I scoffed with a derisive grin, but I composed myself again. "Looking for an uncle we haven't seen in a long time. Wondering if he's still kicking about Boston."

The young librarian tilted her head over to peer at Faith, who was still standing behind me looking up at the ceiling. The librarian said, "You look *very* familiar... Have you and I met before?"

Shit... The news must have our faces everywhere by now...

"I'm Hugh and this is Mia," I said immediately.

"And who are you looking for?"

Faith beamed and piped up, "We're looking for my cousin!"

I shot a glare back at her, which made her withdraw back behind me with a subconscious look in her eyes. I told the librarian, "She hasn't seen her extended family in a long while; we're just wondering if they're still around here..."

The librarian's eyes narrowed at us; I could tell she knew we were lying... but after a sigh, she pushed off the desk, grabbed jangling keys from one of the drawers, and gestured to the other end of the reading hall. "Alright, come on then. Doing something's better than nothing I guess."

. . .

We went back downstairs to the lobby, where the librarian took us to a dusty backroom filled with stacks of mail bins, stacks of paper reams, and a bookshelf filled with binders and other thick contacts books. For some reason, the room was extremely cold; I then looked to my right, and nestled in the corner was a monolith-like mainframe server flanked by three cooling fans. It must have been the entire library's database, but I wasn't curious enough to learn more about it.

There was only the task at hand.

The librarian stood on the tips of her open-toe wedges to reach for the yellow pages at the top right corner of the bookshelf before going to the closest stack of mail bins and setting the book on its lid.

"When you're done, just leave it there and see yourself out."

"Thanks," I said.

Just as she was about to leave the room, I saw out of the corner of my eye that she stopped about half-way through. I looked back and saw that she noticed Faith staring up at the mainframe with curious wonder. The librarian considered her, and I saw something of an amused smile on her face.

"Hey, Mia?" I called, reminding her of her alter ego. "Don't touch that thing, okay?"

The librarian shot a glare at me and, as if to defy me, crouched down to Faith's level and pointed out different things about the server. I could overhear parts of their conversation: She mostly explained how it basically worked and how much power it used. I sighed with concern that Faith might say something that would blow our cover to this stranger, but I was going to have to trust her as I had to focus on finding the only person I could think of who might be able to help her and my brother.

The registry went by surname first, so I flipped the pages to the "L" section; I thought it was uncommon, but I was surprised to see how many people had "Landing" for a surname. As I went down the list, unable to single Phoebe out, I prayed that she didn't get married or became transgender or something; anything that would have changed her name.

Then... I found her...

Phoebe Landing...

I felt the joyous relief fill my chest when I saw it, but I quickly made a note of her phone number before I lost my place. I have a near-eidetic memory, but I wanted to be absolutely sure I would get her number right. I called over to the girls still by the mainframe.

"Fai—Mia!" I called. "Guys, can you get me a pen here? I think I found your cousin."

When none of them responded, I looked at them to see why. The librarian was still crouched at Faith's level, but she was holding her by her shoulders this time while Faith had her small hands pressed against the mainframe... her eyes rolling into the back of her head and her head rocking back and forth while she was repeatedly mumbling something to herself.

I rushed over to Faith's side. "What's wrong?"

The librarian stood up, backing away from us with a concerned look on her face. "She just... put her hands on the mainframe and she got like..." She was still standing over us, holding her hands up as if she didn't know what to do with them. "I'm going to call 911 and see if—"

"No!" I yelled. "This happened before, she was able to snap out of—" I trailed off when I noticed something... something impossible. I couldn't explain it, even now. The mainframe began to light up like a Christmas tree. Ever brighter and brighter, spelling out different flowing patterns that looked floral and kaleidoscopic. The patterns spread over the mainframe... from where Faith had pressed her palms...

CHAPTER 24
FAITH

When I opened my eyes, I looked around and saw that I was suddenly in the middle of a grassy savanna with scattered shrubs and trees, going all the way to mountains at the horizon. I heard crickets and birds chirping all around me. The grass was tall and yellow, reaching up to my hands by my waist.

As confused as I was by this, I heard the grass and trees of this savanna rustle gently; I felt a balmy wind brush through my face and hair; I stood still for a moment, not sure of what to make of all this, but it was peaceful and beautiful. I looked at the red and velvet sunset in front of me, and I had a feeling like I wanted to surrender to something bigger than myself.

I closed my eyes and just... was...

But then I heard a snarling sound that made me open my eyes again. I looked at the grass ahead of me, at first seeing nothing, then... two glowing-white eyes, watching me carefully and coming closer. At first, I thought it was a lion or a tiger, but when I saw its snout, I saw two teeth the size of kitchen knives coming out. I immediately froze up, unsure of whether I wanted to run or scream even though I knew doing either would have maybe excited the saber-toothed cat. But just as the cat was about to pounce on me...

I heard what sounded like screaming chimpanzees behind me. Only, they twice as large as any chimp I had ever seen. They came next to me, beating the dirt and pounding their chests as a way to stick together and scare away the cat. I stumbled back away from the cat, scrambling for cover behind the apes. The cat looked like it was beginning to lose its nerve, but it wasn't backing down quite yet; many times, it tried to lunge for my legs.

My heart raced in my throat as I watched these apes pick up sharp stones from the ground... and stand upright on two legs.

These apes moved against the cat, throwing the stones at the cat as it backed away from them, still trying to single me out from them. The stones pelted the earth around the cat, and it wasn't until one hit the cat's spotted hide that it finally ran off into the distance with its tail between its legs. The apes chased after it, throwing more stones to make sure that the cat would stay away. I was still on the ground, putting a hand on my chest to calm down my heart and slow down my breaths.

I then heard a familiar voice behind me say, *"Ecce Homo..."*

I knew that voice...

I tried not to panic and scream with joy. My heart raced faster, and I couldn't hold it anymore. I looked up at Hugo standing over me, looking at the apes with a smile on his face. I wanted with all of my heart to leap up and throw myself into his arms. He hadn't changed at all. He was still wearing his favorite denim jacket, and his blonde hair was as long and wild as it was the day he left us.

The only thing I thought was different was his blue eyes; something in them changed... like he made peace with something, and he hasn't been so sure of something in his whole life. As I felt tears come into my eyes, I followed his eyes back to the apes to share in the thing that has been giving him life ever since he died.

Through my breaking voice, I asked him, "What are they?"

"No, not 'what.' Who!" Hugo answered. "They are your 2-million-year-old relatives. Remarkable, aren't they? Like something straight out of your *Spore* video game."

But there was still something I still didn't understand. I stood back up and went up to Hugo, clinging onto the clothes over his chest and wedging my cheek deeper into his heart so I could hear its beating. I shut my eyes and asked him, "What is this place, Hugo?"

He didn't answer me. He just kept quiet, watching the horizon like it was a painting. I didn't look up at him; I just wanted to feel his warmth... because I knew this moment wasn't real. I was in his world, not mine. But the longer I stayed hugging him, the more I felt something in my surroundings change. I felt the ground beneath my feet changing. I felt the sun and the stars spiral around the Earth like a clock hand, and I felt the air bringing new elements across the landscape. New rivers, new mountains, new trees, new animals...

When I opened my eyes again, I saw that the entire world seemed to be accelerating. The sun rose and set within seconds, and each time it rose and set, it looked like Hugo and I were standing in a very different place and a different time.

The sun set and rose, and there was snow. Cavemen wearing fur coats, holding spears and torches as they walked along a migrating herd of Woolly Mammoths overlooking a steep cliff. The sun set and rose, and there was an oasis in the desert. Tribes farming with water, building homes out of rocks and wood, and dragging wheelbarrows. The sun set and rose faster and faster now, and I saw pyramids rising from the sands, temples being built to sun gods, walls being built through forests.

The sun set and rose, and I saw ancient- and medieval-looking men in robes drawing and building bigger cities and discovering newer things in science and math; I saw the smokestacks and clock towers and churches of Europe; I saw the cranes and brick build- ings and glass skyscrapers of Boston; I saw two comets *rising* from the Earth, racing each other to the moon to explore where no man had ever gone before...

Then the sun set... but this time, it never rose... I tried looking around, but there was nothing but complete darkness and silence. Hugo wasn't there with me anymore, and my hands were still clenched into fists where I was holding his clothes. I couldn't feel the ground beneath my feet. I couldn't feel what was up, down, left, or right. This "place" didn't feel right... None of this felt right.

Then the silence asked me what I was doing and why I was resisting.

"Hugo?" I called. "Is that you? Where are you?"

The silence answered that he was still here. It asked if I couldn't see him.

"No, I can't see you!"

Then... more silences came to me, and I shook my head to keep them out. They were all telling me that Hugo wasn't supposed to bring me here, and that I knew it. Hugo was never meant to find them, but he couldn't help himself and wanted to taste the forbidden fruit and learn the universe's secrets before humanity was ready to understand... and accept...

I heard Hugo's silence beg me to not listen to them and to come with him. I didn't know what I wanted... I did want to be with him, but not like this... I felt like I was at the edge of something so vast and so awful... a wormhole so dangerous and powerful that if I stepped over, I would never see the world I knew ever again... I wasn't so sure if I wanted to take that step and see what Hugo was seeing... but I reached my hand out into the darkness for him, wondering if he'd reach out to me too...

"Hugo..." I said. "Just come back to me, please... Mom and I miss you so much..."

The silence just told me to come with him... To see humanity's next step towards its destiny... To see the Truth... To see *them*...

CHAPTER 25
LEVI

Faith looked like she was possessed by some demon, and her mind seemed to have been shackled to the mainframe. I didn't know what to do. I just kept shaking her by the shoulders, trying to rip her away from it. But it seemed like the more I tried, the more the mainframe rattled and smoldered as the cables shot out from the power supply and patterns of multi-colored lights continued to swim up and down its LED display. The fluorescent lights above me buzzed and flickered as if a tornado was coming our way. I looked back at the librarian, who looked just as confused and horrified as I was.

I tried again. "Faith! Faith, snap out of it! Wake up!"

"What is this, Hugh?" I heard the librarian whisper.

"Faith! Wake up!"

"Hugh!"

I snapped back at the librarian. "What is it!?"

She wasn't looking at me. The look in her eyes as

she was watching something on the mainframe... It was as if another nightmare had fallen upon her. I followed her eyes back to the mainframe, and I noticed a new pattern was taking shape, materializing into a series of letters and symbols. It looked like some kind of arithmetic function, but there wasn't anything logical about it; it didn't have any rhyme or reason to it:

$$\textbf{P=NP}$$
$$\|$$
$$\textbf{(x OR y OR z) AND (x OR }\bar{\textbf{y}}\textbf{ OR z) AND}$$
$$\textbf{(x OR y OR }\bar{\textbf{z}}\textbf{) AND (x OR }\bar{\textbf{y}}\textbf{ OR }\bar{\textbf{z}}\textbf{) AND}$$
$$\textbf{(}\bar{\textbf{x}}\textbf{ OR y OR z) AND (}\bar{\textbf{x}}\textbf{ OR }\bar{\textbf{y}}\textbf{ OR }\bar{\textbf{z}}\textbf{)}\ =\ 1$$

But somehow, the function kept growing and expanding outwards. It wasn't until more versions of the same functions spread across the mainframe that it finally short-circuited with a small explosion; the single flaring spark severed whatever connection Faith had with the server. She shot up to her feet and immediately lost her balance, stumbling back against me.

I caught her by her underarms and she held onto me with a grip that clutched tightly like a vice. She was shaking uncontrollably, as if she had just narrowly survived a freezing winter. I tried to stand her up by her shoulders, but her head kept going limp and her eyes were fading. She was clearly about to faint.

I could only hear her mutter one thing: "What is the Truth, Hugo?"

I gathered her to my chest and held her up by her shoulders, hoping she had at least enough strength to use me as a crutch to hobble out of the library. I looked back at the mainframe to see the damage she left behind; I still couldn't believe what I had just seen. *Was this like what happened to Hugo? How? She wasn't even wearing a BCI!* I was more relieved that Faith wasn't killed, but I wasn't sure if the experience left any lasting damage to her brain. The librarian was still standing there, looking incredulously at the now-defunct mainframe.

I whispered to Faith, trying to reassure her. "Faith, just stay with me. We're gonna go find a phone and find Phoebe. She's got to be somewhere out—"

Then, I heard the librarian call out to us, "Phoebe Landing?"

I froze in my tracks and slowly, as if moving underwater, I turned back towards the librarian who was still quietly pondering over the mainframe. She turned to meet my gaze, just as shocked as I was to find her here of all places...

"Oh, shit," I muttered in disbelief.

CHAPTER 26
FAITH

I woke up extremely cold and sweaty. I had a really bad headache. My eyes felt heavy, and I tried to keep them open to see where I was now. I wasn't in the library anymore. I was lying in someone's bedroom. There were dirty clothes all around the carpeted floor, and there was only one large window to my left to let in the blue moonlight. I heard a staticky sound across the room from me. It was a small TV playing the news.

I saw my face and Levi's on it, with the words MISSING and DANGEROUS scrolling across the screen. The next shot was an bird's-eye view of a large gray building surrounded by large crowds and police officers... I sat up to look closer at the familiar-looking building.

My heart beat faster when I realized that it was the Boston Public Library.

I heard another sound coming from inside the walls in another room somewhere. One of the doors down the hall in front of me flew open, and a shirtless man stormed in, followed by the librarian we met earlier today. She was chasing him to the bathroom, yelling for him to leave her apartment while also yelling a ton of bad words at him. Following in behind her was Levi, whose eyes widened when he saw me. He rushed to my bedside, pressed a hand against my forehead, and looked straight into my eyes.

He then asked me, "What's the last thing you remember?"

I thought way too hard for such an easy question. I shut my eyes and gulped out, "I, uh... I was in that room looking at that shelf of lights... Oh, Levi, I feel so dizzy... What happened?"

We both jumped at the bathroom door flying open. The librarian was still screaming at the man until he finally ran down the hall and left with his bag and clothes in his arms. Levi then gently pushed my shoulders back down on the bed and pulled the covers over me to tuck me in. "A lot's happened since then. I'll explain to you later, but right now, you should get some rest. You've been through a lot."

Then the librarian turned her anger on Levi. "How about you explain it to *me* now!? What was all of that!?"

"You're not even interested in catching up with your cousin, Phoebe?" he asked. "It's been so long, you barely even recognized each other back at the library."

"Yeah, well, fake names don't sit well at family reunions."

I immediately sat up to look right at her and asked, "Wait. Phoebe? *You're* Phoebe?"

"And you're both popular," she said. She picked

up the TV remote from a nearby coffee table and unmuted the TV before throwing it back down.

The news lady talking in the background said, "—*the Department of Defense has called for a nationwide manhunt for 17-year-old Levi Abd al-Rahman, the younger brother of the formerly acclaimed M.I.T. computer neuroscientist and global futurist Enoch Abd al-Rahman. This morning, Levi is believed to have kidnapped 11-year-old Faith Landing in her home in Newbridge. Faith is the younger sister of Hugo Landing, who was killed in an accident caused by Enoch Abd al-Rahman's newly designed virtual reality goggles, the BCI.4.*

"Newbridge County law enforcement claims that they have reason to suspect that the two children are in possession of highly sensitive intelligence about brain-computer interface technology in connection to Hugo's death, though for what reason is still not yet certain. A leaked report from the DoD reveals that the two brothers' father was a member of the PFLP, or the Popular Front for the Liberation of Palestine, a U.S.-designated communist terrorist organization founded by the Christian Palestinian revolutionary George Habash. If anyone has any information on the whereabouts of the fugitives—"

Phoebe switched off the TV, looking at both of us as if we had to explain ourselves. I didn't know what to say; I just lifted the covers over my nose, worriedly peering over to see what her next reaction would be. Levi just stood there, meeting her angry eyes with his angry eyes.

"Phoebe, listen to me..." Levi said.

"So is it true?" she demanded.

"It's a very long story."

"Go ahead and try me."

"You wouldn't believe me; *I* still don't believe it."

"Believe *what?*"

Then Levi added with a sigh, "Phoebe, please, I—I'm into something here I cannot understand."

"That *you* can't understand!?" Phoebe scoffed. "You're incredible, you know that? I just saw *my cousin* here, who looks like she *just* started middle school, beginning to solve the most impossible computer science problem in history while also talking to her dead brother, who, I should add, I was playing video games with not even four months ago! She overrode thousands upon thousands of dollars worth of giga-bytes *using only her mind;* that mainframe paid my bills and kept me fed after your brother got me canned from M.I.T.! Do you have any idea how hard it was for me to land that job to archive and digitize books for the library? And now, you've both *quite literally* blown it for me!"

Levi muttered, "Well, you were caught stealing from my brother, so..."

"And speaking of your brother," Phoebe contin-ued, "I come home with his brother and his victim's little sister, then I turn on the news and hear *his* name being mentioned in the same sentence as the Morris worm! 'National security threat level,' they said. So yeah, try me, Levi. I think I'm now entitled to try to understand everything about the mess I've just gotten myself into..."

Levi kept quiet for a while, and I could see that he

still couldn't make up his mind about telling her about whatever it was that happened back at the library. He looked back at me, and his hardened stare softened before walking towards his backpack on the floor beneath the window. He took out his journal, and with it, he pointed down the hall.

"Look, Faith here really needs her rest," Levi said. "She's also been through a lot today... and I think we should both sit down for this. Maybe we should take this to the kitchen."

"Alright, fine," Phoebe scoffed. "This had better be good."

"Oh, you just wait," he retorted dryly. "Some of it is *literally* out of this world."

CHAPTER 27
LEVI

I told Phoebe what happened in the museum, what happened this morning, and why we're here now. I left out the practically inconsequential fact that Hugo's mother destroyed his BCI since Enoch told me that it made her look bad to whatever shadow agency arrested her and, after Phoebe saw my family's connection to terrorist activities on TV, I had a feeling she might take it the wrong way and think that his mom and I were colluding to try to cover something up. I only told Phoebe that Hugo's mother was taken in for interrogation, but that's all I knew.

Even so, against my better judgment, even after everything Phoebe had done against my brother, I gave her his journal. His life was at stake and, apparently, so was Faith's. After she finished reading through every page, she just sat there and had this shell-shocked look on her face as she chewed on the impossible truth. At times, she looked up from the book and stared around the room, probably wondering if anyone else was seeing what was in the book.

"So..." I ventured, "what do you think about all this?"

Phoebe scoffed. "Are you seriously kidding me? You and Faith might as well have just handed me the newest clue to the alchemical stone."

I gave her a perplexed look. "Why?"

She turned the book over and pointed at a diagram of the BCI.4; above it was that same formula we saw back at the library: P=NP. "You have no idea what this means, do you?"

"Am I supposed to?"

"No, but frankly, I'm not sure I'm supposed to either. No one is."

I shook my head at her. "Phoebe, c'mon, cut the beautiful mind crap. What's with that formula exactly?"

She frantically flipped a page over and set the book down on the kitchen table. "C'mere, take a look at this. You see that?" She pointed to a familiar looking pattern. My heart thumped in my chest when I recognized it: The very same logical functions that appeared on the mainframe back in the library *(x OR y OR z)*.

She continued, "That is a Propositional Satisfiability Problem. In logic and computer science, it is a problem with a given set of variables with truth values that negate one another, organized between the logic gates AND and OR such that some permutations would make the theorem required to solve it satisfiable, or equal to one, and others unsatisfiable, or undefined."

I shrugged my shoulders. "Okay, but what exactly is so special about it?"

"With this problem? Nothing," Phoebe answered, "which is exactly the idea. It's *supposed* to be unremarkable; a mathematical principle that is universal in its nature."

I shot her a puzzled look. "What do you mean?"

"It is one of countless problems designated as 'NP-Complete.' A class of increasingly complex problems that only a nondeterministic polynomial-time algorithm can find every last solution to. For conventional computers, the number of machine operations to solve a problem increases relative to input or question size. That means that NP-Complete problems would take our normal, 'brute force' computer algorithms a seemingly infinite exponential number of code-breaking operations to find every last solution to through randomized 'guessing'—a process that can take an impractical amount of time even with smaller inputs —, though, in retrospect, they take virtually no time to verify that they're true after they've been solved."

"I didn't understand a single word of what you just said, Phoebe," I said, crossing my arms.

Phoebe looked bristled by my remark. She slammed the book shut and walked towards me as if I had personally offended her. "The class of problems that we right now consider to be computable in exponential time share the fundamental properties that they are easy to verify in retrospect and that no proof faster than a brute force 'guessing' one has been found to solve them, meaning that each and every one of these problems are equally reducible to one another in difficulty. Solving the solution to *only one* of these problems—a master problem—within a set number of functions means that we will have mathematically solved this abstract concept of 'guessing,' meaning that we can actually solve *every single problem* within a set number of functions.

"The main problem is finding a new method to solve the same exponential-time problems we've always had to deal with... and the solution to this problem is conclusively determining that there can't possibly be any more solutions to it. Solving an extremely difficult jigsaw puzzle can become just as easy as verifying that all the pieces fit together correctly. No matter how big the input size is, the exponent representing the number of nested machine operations required to solve the problem *doesn't grow*, and the problem is solved within a fixed amount of time regardless of the equation's complexity.

"All problems 'NP' as difficult and complex as stock market projections and cancer-causing protein folding can become just as easy and predictable as kindergarten-level 'P' sorting and multiplication. If P=NP, then we will no longer have to 'guess' our way towards the answers to some of life's greatest questions. And the beautiful thing about polynomial time? Because all instances of NP-Completeness are equally difficult, a master problem can be *any* NP-Complete problem! Propositional Satisfiability, Bijective Graph Isomorphism, Maximal Cliques, Spatial Reasoning, Sudoku, Rubik's Cubes, even something like finding the fastest way to beat an 8-bit *Super Mario* level on the very first playthrough!"

I still couldn't believe what I was hearing: *A single*

mathematics proof that can solve virtually every problem humanity has ever had to face?

But while I was still reeling from this revelation, Phoebe added, "And Faith could have only learned the proof from either Hugo... or aliens..."

Now I feel that I have lost my sanity: Phoebe was saying exactly what Faith said happened to *her* back at the cove. She was actually claiming that Faith got this math proof either from Hugo or an alien life form. Even after a whole hour, I kept asking her to explain herself, but she only came back with the same answer: "I'm not saying that's what actually happened, but that's the only causal explanation I could think of that fits. *Nothing* on Earth is that powerful!"

I came close to yelling. "And you think Faith talked with ghosts and aliens? Is that your considered hypothesis? Faith's a *child,* and her brother died right in her arms. That has to have an effect on someone's impressionable psyche. Maybe her brain was just telling her she was seeing Hugo or aliens as a way to try to cope with what was actually happening to her brain."

"Hey, why don't you cool it with the Batman persona for a minute, would you?" she spat. "I'm not saying that I know for a fact what she thought she saw. You're right: Something clearly happened at Faith's house this morning that made her think she reestablished some kind of connection to Hugo. She could have seen anything. After all, she went into *his* room and put on *his* BCI. But right after that, government agents showed up unannounced at your home."

"It's like the news said: Our father was part of a terro—"

Phoebe cut me off. "I know you don't believe that's the reason, Levi. They would've arrested you a lot sooner before Hugo died. Why in the world is the *government* so interested in her? Why did all of this happen to *her* and not you or Enoch? That little girl in my bedroom... What I saw back in the library was a little girl solving an impossible math problem on the belief that she was talking to her dead brother.

"As powerful as it is, the mainframe isn't that powerful; the only way she could have done that is if she exploited nonlinearities in time and space at the quantum scale beyond even what our modern super-computers are capable of. And there is no way she could have done it... without the help of some *higher* intelligence... A consciousness..."

"A consciousness from where?" I demanded.

"Within," she answered.

"What do you mean wi—" I broke off as the realization completely seized my mind. I looked around my surroundings, beginning to wonder if any of what I was seeing or hearing or experiencing was even reality anymore.

First contact... with a parallel dimension?

"Maybe that day in the museum when Hugo died, he didn't really die," Phoebe continued, just as unsettled by the realization. "His mind must have... transitioned to some place beyond our world. A new world beyond what we're capable of sensing. And after seeing what he saw, he's reaching back out to the only connection he has left in the real world to tell us what it is..."

For a moment, I considered the possibility. The

lunacy of such an idea. I paced away, rubbing my face up to my forehead until I stopped at the window, watching the night sky and wondering if *he* was up there among the heavens, looking down on me.

Looking down on Faith...

Then Phoebe added, "But even if Hugo's still alive... *impossibly* alive... that still doesn't explain how he got the proof in the first place; he had to have gotten it from somewhere or someone or something else. And judging by the way this conversation is going, I don't think you've ever talked about NP-Completeness with him?"

I shook my head, still taking in the full measure of her claims. "But how... how could Faith even exploit *quantum* phenomena beyond what our computers can do?"

Then I heard Phoebe sigh out, "To solve a computational complexity theory as arcane and forbidding as NP-Completeness, you're gonna need a nondeterministic processor that can prescribe multiple, seemingly infinite programs *in parallel*—without having it being governed by a previous computer state—within a fixed timeframe to account for *every last* branching path of a given problem. A computer processor like that would either require more energy than the sun or the exploitation of quantum phenomena! But there is only one place in the universe I can think of that is capable of dilating time and energy in this manner... the ultimate limit of computational complexity..."

"Where?" I asked.

"Your brother wrote in his journal's addendum that he doesn't want to believe it... but that there is no other possible explanation..." After a brief pause, Phoebe finally answered, "The only possible place in the universe where the laws of relativity and quantum mechanics might be reconciled..."

As her words hung in the air, the realization dawned like a sudden burst of blinding light. I felt something in my mind beginning to unravel, and I felt my heart wavering between incomprehension, terror, and wonder. *So that is what my brother came to realize? That is what Faith saw and what all of this has been building up to?*

"A Black Hole?" I said aloud.

"If the NP-Complete proof is the pearl, the Black Hole's Singularity is the clam."

"How is that even possible?"

Phoebe held my brother's journal tight in her hands. "It's so intricate, yet so simple... Your brother saw something in humanity's own evolution. As he saw it, transhumanism is an inevitability; most, if not all, of humanity will have their consciousness 'uploaded' to some technological cloud through virtual reality and artificial intelligence. The happenstance circumstances of most peoples' lives will be trumped by the hope for a metaversal utopia. But it won't stop there. As our computers' processing power becomes more advanced, it increasingly becomes more complex and efficient while using much less time and energy.

"We've already seen through Moore's Law and Koomey's Law that the number of computer transistors doubles every two years while the number of computer operations per joule of energy used also doubles every two years. We're already making breakthroughs in quantum computing; it isn't hard to believe that we will one day compute all the way down to the $10^{-35\text{th}}$ order of magnitude. As our computers miniaturize and accelerate towards quantum space, they compress and densify in space, time, energy, and matter..."

I soon realized where Phoebe was taking this. I contributed, "And with Albert Einstein's mass-energy equivalence principle, $E=MC^2$, energy is equivalent to matter. And because all things with mass and energy have their own gravity, the more dense mass and energy become..."

Phoebe finished, "...the more time and space become curved around it. And as gravity alters the fabric of the space-time continuum around high-mass objects, there also exists a link between gravitation and the way in which the universe's many substrates 'metabolize' information. Our ever-advancing computational systems are becoming more localized and miniaturized, increasingly compressing space, time, energy, and matter alike down to one single point. Digitized computer bits will replace physical atoms and computer software will replace physical actions. As complexity densifies space, time, energy, and matter, it also dematerializes them, accelerating them at an exponential rate to a density beyond even the nano- and pico-scales: A *femto*-scale domain..."

"But all the way down to a Black Hole Singularity?" I finally concluded. "Do you even know how much gravity it would take to reach that level of density?"

"I know that a Black Hole the size of a peanut

would have the same weight and gravity as the Earth. Not to mention the 367 billion mile Phoenix Cluster Black Hole has the mass of *20 billion of our suns!*" Phoebe straightened, and I could see that she was starting to realize the absurdity of such a conclusion. "Maybe it isn't *exactly* a Black Hole Singularity per se, but its behavior certainly resembles it. What else could it be?"

I scoffed. "So you're telling me that either Hugo or aliens have been talking to Faith from inside a Black Hole-like environment somewhere out there all this time without even—"

"I don't think you're understanding me," Phoebe interrupted. "They're not inside a 'Black Hole...' They *are* the Black Hole... They have *become* the Black Hole... Maybe what happened to Hugo that day wasn't an accident. Maybe it was just us reaching out to a destiny that we weren't meant to realize yet... But that doesn't mean that other forms of intelligent life haven't realized theirs already, which is why we haven't found them yet..."

I didn't know what she meant at first, but the longer I stared at her, the more the revelation sank in. I walked towards her with a half-turned face, still not sure if I entirely believed what Phoebe was getting at. I then offered, "Are you saying that if we go beyond biology... there's a chance we also go beyond existence itself?"

Phoebe shook her head incredulously, unsure if she could bring herself to believe it also. "It seems to be the perfect answer to Fermi's Paradox: The contradiction between the sheer size of the universe, the high statistical probability that life should emerge, and the complete lack of evidence for it. There should be galactic empires and interstellar alliances all over the universe, but as far as we know, there are no clear-cut biological or technological signatures on other planets. Why is the universe so quiet?"

"It's that we all disappear into a dimension outside of space and time through a technological singularity?"

"We're already seeing the beginning of the 'mind-uploading' transhumanist age; the hybridization between biology and technology is increasing at an exponential rate with every new age, and biological intelligence and Black Holes represent the two most complex known informational substrates in the universe.

"Once the complexity of consciousness intersects with and compounds the complexity of quantum mechanics through our computational abilities, time will no longer be perceived by consciousness in minutes or seconds, but in the number of code-breaking operations necessary to understand every corner of the universe.

"And if the Sapir-Whorf hypothesis is true—that the language we speak determines our underlying perception of the world—, then our learning a completely new and foreign 'language' will dramatically rewire how our brains will categorize our human paradigm of existence. We will experience another side of the unchanged reality that we never knew always existed.

"And due to the gravitational redshift dilating our collective perception of time and space within a Black

Hole Singularity, we will all merge seemingly instantaneously at the end of time. Within that redshift, it is only a matter of time before at least one of the trillions of intelligent species out there exploits quantum phenomena to find an NP-Complete algorithm that can solve any input it is given in virtually no time—and I do mean *no time.* No relative local time.

"All of this is to say that every intelligent life form in the universe that is capable of technological progress will, in their own time, find a way to perpetuate consciousness after physical death by transcending the space-time continuum towards the ultimate limit of computation: Transcension."

I walked back towards the window to look back up at the stars. Only this time, now, I knew... I knew that he was up there somewhere... I then looked down the hall to see Faith lying in bed, her eyes staring out the window as if still searching for her brother. I understood... but as startling as Phoebe's conclusions were, I didn't feel any closer to understanding what we ought to do next. How to save our families. How to protect Faith.

Then, as if reading my mind, Phoebe broke the silence. "Ahhh.... Shit... I think I have a plan, but I don't think either of you are gonna like it..."

CHAPTER 28
LEVI

Every day, I remember the past that I wish I could just forget, and each time I remember, I shut my eyes and hope that the living nightmare would be over soon. But I have carried that nightmare in my heart... I remember my childhood in a small Christian Palestinian town in the West Bank called Beit Jala. I don't think I could even call it a childhood.

In the areas surrounding my home, there were mobs wearing bandanas throwing rocks and shooting at armored riot police in the trash-strewn streets, setting fire to overturned cars, fleeing from flashbangs and tear gas. At night, there was the muffled crackling of gunfire, but for me, these sounds of war never really came that close to my home; I therefore paid little mind to them, almost as if they were nothing more than the everyday sounds of construction work.

But my dad was a part of that world. He chose to fight with the soldiers and the rioters. He wasn't home a lot ever since mom died... Now that I think of it, it never really felt like home... Enoch was the only home I had ever known. He was always there for me when I didn't know what was going on around me.

I can't remember much of what happened and he wouldn't tell me what it meant, but when he won his scholarship from M.I.T. after going to the Technion in Haifa, he didn't even tell dad that we were leaving them for a world outside the violence. We just quickly packed our things and ran away to Boston before we could get sucked into our father's life...

I remember the last thing I saw when the plane took off. I saw the Dome of the Rock; the crown jewel of the Holy Land; the last place where men were said to have talked to beings from the heavens; the place from which God created the universe; the Holy of Holies that housed His truth... and its golden dome shone over Jerusalem like the blinding light of the unconquered sun...

I opened my eyes... and even in the dead of night, I found myself still blinded by that same unconquered sun: The golden dome of the Massachusetts State House. I was sitting with my legs dangling from the fire escape landing outside Phoebe's bedroom window, resting my elbows on one of the emergency ladder's rungs as I brooded in melancholic solitude.

It wasn't complete solitude as the city's night life was still far from quiet; car klaxons, emergency sirens, rap music thumping out of passing cars, planes roaring overhead from Logan Airport. But after I blocked out all that noise, I contemplated the State House's dome shining in the moonlight between federal and financial high-rises, nearly crowded out by billboards for law firms, insurance companies, car dealerships, Big Tech web apps, fashion, cosmetics, fast food, and block-buster movies and video games.

All there is to do in the world... is consume...

The way we're consuming everything now, I dreaded to think how we'd act as one Black Hole. Even so, I always believed that, one day, even with all this consumerism, humanity will come to uncover every-thing there is to know about the universe; the idea that everything that can be scientifically known *will* be known, I've always taken for granted and taken comfort in. After all, we've somehow managed to find a way to calculate the entire perimeter of a circle from the arc of just a tiny segment.

For all of our failures as a species and for all of God's silence, I thought that we at least can be rest assured by the fact that, one day, justice and truth will inevitably win out in the end somehow. But now, I know that *they* are out there somewhere. Sentient Black Holes watching over us, lying in wait beyond what we are capable of scientifically understanding.

But Phoebe told me that Black Holes are more than destroyers of worlds that consume everything in their path. They existed 700 million years after the Big Bang, not to mention Supermassive Black Holes are the core of most galaxies. They may assort the funda-mental physical parameters of the universe, but they themselves don't stand outside of them. However incomprehensible they might be, they are just as much a creature as the sun and other stars. They simply lie right between the forces of creation and destruction, making them the loci of what gives existence its exis-tence: An invisible, mysterious reality without a name that goes beyond any subatomic particles, and is more of a verb than a noun. A hidden code in inner space, embedded in the quantum fabric of the universe.

Not gods, but apocalyptic prophets that channel His "Word."

But then there is also that invisible "light" by which we see and understand that "verbing" reality without a name. For the evolutionary neuroscientist, there is the "Binding Problem," which is the human illusion of some fixed, objective "meaning" of the universe made of some long-forgotten primordial event in our history; a missing link in our evolutionary psychology where raw phenomena took form in our minds. For the linguist, there is the "Hermeneutic Circle," which is the idea that to truly understand the true meaning of any one part, we have to know how the parts are connected to the whole; and to understand the whole, we have to understand how each and every individual part works. For the existentialist, it's that impenetrable, timeless mystery of "Being."

Either way, at some point in our evolutionary history, a rock, a tree, and a cloud *became* a rock, a tree, and a cloud in all our subconsciouses, and that reality without a name became "divided up" and "disguised" to us as rocks, trees, and clouds, as if they have always existed.

So if our final destination really is an outside of space and time... an outside of even the universe's "verbing" phenomena, where everything that there is to know about this universe will one day be known... will it truly be the fulfillment of our own sense of existence or will it be its complete annihilation? As we accelerate our change and transcend reality, will we realize our own nature or abandon it altogether?

Maybe this was all some new gnostic alchemy after all. If everything we see is just an illusion, then we really should "visit the interior of the Earth, and by rectification, find the Hidden Stone." The long-sought secret that would finally make us all immortal and allow us to talk to beings from the heavens.

As I wondered this, I had this uneasy sense that those beings were monitoring me, as they always have been ever since the foundation of the world. Contrary to popular understanding, Black Hole Singularities are not a specific point in space at the center of the Event Horizon, but a final future point in history. As we approach them, time itself accelerates to the end of the universe, where all that exists will merge together in one final endpoint; an essence that is a literal "Being-towards-Death"; prophets of an apocalyptic communion. If it is true that they have already transcended, and that we will make contact with them at the end of all time... then to them...

To them, we have already communed with them and they with us countless ages ago... We just haven't realized it yet...

Hugo, I have always been your best friend... If you really are alive, tell me now: Is this proof that you showed your sister going to renew us or destroy us?

I then heard the window slide open behind me. I turned around and saw Faith climb up to the landing with me, her red bed sheet wrapped around her head and shoulders like a cowl. She stood there for a moment, as if to ask my permission for something; I looked her up and down, unsure of how to react to her being here with me. I didn't say anything. I just leaned back on my hands and gazed back out towards the city skyline, still figuring out my role in this new world I now found myself in.

Out of the corner of my eye, I saw Faith come up beside me. With her bed sheet still wrapped around her, she sat down on the grating with her back leaned against the railing next to me and her knees hugged to her chest. She didn't join me in staring out at the city; she just stared down at her knees, quiet and withdrawn into herself. I wasn't sure what to say to break the silence, but before I could think of something, I felt her small hand slide over my fingers on the grating.

I looked over and saw a dapple of blue moonlight slash down across her delicate face, framed in shadow and set against the darkness as if disembodied. In her drained eyes, it wasn't only sadness and exhaustion I saw, but she looked... lost... She was bleeding internally, desperately trying to piece back together the shattered fragments of the life she once knew... and I didn't know how to feel about being the only lifeline she had left in her life.

"Levi..." she finally said, "what were you talking with Phoebe in the kitchen about?"

"We were trying to understand what happened to you back at the library."

"And what did she say?"

I sighed out, "We don't know... Some kind of code that might be able to 'infiltrate' real life."

"A code?"

"Kinda, but not like Skynet or the Matrix. It's not

a *computer* code per se, but it's something invisible that touches everything in the universe; it might even be able to change the way reality works."

"Like the Force in *Star Wars?*" Faith offered.

I was going to say no at first, but I soon recognized where her question was coming from. I knew that she never obsessed over those movies the way Hugo and I did; if anything, I think she hated them for directing so much attention away from her. But she knew those movies and games were his favorite pastime.

I then turned the idea over in my head and considered that maybe there might have been something to it after all. I answered tenderly, "Sure... like the Force—"

"Are you still mad at me, Levi?"

I frowned at her. "Mad at you? For what?"

Her voice returned timidly. "For everything. For not stopping us from going into the museum room. For ruining your life. If you hate me, it's okay, but please, I need to know."

I sighed and shook my head at her. "No. I'm not mad. I've never been mad. I've never hated you. And there is nothing to forgive."

"Okay..." she said, her meek voice emerging through a choked whimper. "Because I think mom is still mad at me for ruining hers. I know she loves me... and she knows what's best for me... But I think Hugo and I got her into more trouble now..." She started to sniffle and her eyes became misty until a shimmer of moonlight streamed down her cheek. She pressed the heels of her palms against her eyes to ease the overwhelming strain on her mind.

Though I knew Faith to be clumsy and naive ever

since I met Hugo, there was a certain gentle grace that she carried herself with. I took this as mostly a weakness, but I recognized that there was something about that attitude that stubbornly endured even though everyone and everything was changing around her.

But something did change in Faith today, and I realized that I didn't help to stop it. My heart was broken when Hugo died, and I refused to open it up more. But seeing Faith's spirit crumbling like this without anyone left to trust, I admitted with difficulty, "The reason I have not been talking to you at school is because I felt like I was the one who took your brother away from you... and I couldn't bear looking at you because every time I saw your eyes, I saw his..."

Faith sucked in a breath and hid her face in her bedsheet. She stared distantly as she turned inward and ruminated on something else: "When my dad died, I only had Hugo to show me the world. He shaped the whole world for me. But then he died, and I felt like I lost a part of myself in him. I feel so lost without him... and I want to say sorry to mom that I still exist. I'm so scared to die, Levi... but the whole world is mad at me for killing Hugo. I want to be with him in Heaven... and no one down here would ever know that I left."

Her words struck me like nothing I have ever felt before. This was beyond any pity I had ever seen or felt before in my life. "You didn't kill Hugo, and it wasn't your fau—" I had already gotten tired of listening to myself before I even finished saying that sentence. She's heard this a million times from our counselor, and if I was this sick of hearing that argument over and over again, I could have only imagined how she felt. I knew that nothing that I could ever say could help lift the weight bearing down on her will to go on.

A heaviness gripped my heart, and I was paralyzed by the realization of how much of a piece of shit I was to her all this time with her harboring so much suffering in her soul... and still strong enough to quietly endure through it all. I could only think to offer her one thing, no matter how painful it was to admit it to both her and to myself.

"When my brother got accepted into M.I.T.," I said, "he brought us here for the hope of a better future so that we might actualize ourselves and make something meaningful of our lives. We went from the so-called 'Promised Land' to the 'City on a Hill.' After all, the spirit of the American Revolution was born here; a spirit to break free from the tyranny and religion of the old world to try to create a new, united utopia... *E pluribus unum,*' as the Founding Fathers put on our money of all places. 'Out of many, one.' But now that I think about it, at what cost? There have been countless genocides and colonizations born from that delusion, robbing them of the right to realize what they were created to be.

"And ever since Enoch and I came here, I noticed the same problem. I've only seen people trying to be something they're not. Buying into reactionary ideologies to virtue signal, buying and showing off meaningless cars and jewelry on social media, clouting body images and work ethics, all because we see others do the exact same thing and go along with it just so that we can believe in some illusion of real change. People crave social proofs and bandwagon for the sake of bandwagoning. It was then that I learned and accepted that no matter where we go or what we do or who we are... we will never feel at home with ourselves in the world.

"If you go along with whatever the mobs in society expect from you, you will feel so far removed from your own sense of self until, one day, you'll finally believe it and you fully lose sight of who you are... As you sell your soul to society's fast-paced, never-ending rat races and hurry from one little task to another, all that is left of you is an uncomfortable certainty that you will never be what you could have been.

"But if you want to stay true to yourself... you become terrified that you will be left behind and forgotten by everyone. So you lock yourself away from the real world into some kind of echo chamber as you try to distract yourself from that possibility until, one day, all that is left of you is an uncomfortable certainty that you will never be what you could have been.

"We will always find a way to exist outside of the real world and outside of ourselves. It's all a cruel catch-22. If you surrender, you define yourself by what other people are. But if you fight, you define yourself by what you think you're not, and end up fixating on what other people are. You don't stop and think to find who *you* really are. Instead, we will always feel..."

"Alienated?" Faith offered.

I looked over at her. She was looking at me with a sad, but understanding look on her face. I then pointed to all the buildings in front of us and went on, "So long as our pride and wants escalate, our progress accelerates. We will build more cities, create robots, and raise people from the dead. Society will always find new ways to craft and perpetuate lies about who you are supposed to be to fit its own selfish ideas of progress; you start thinking that you want what it wants until it becomes hard to distinguish reality from the illusions that other people make for us... or the illusions we make for ourselves..."

"So who I think I am..." Faith said, "is not who I actually am?"

"That's only for you to find out, not me." When I saw the look of desperation in Faith's eyes, I realized now why Hugo tried his best to keep us separate. Everything I've told her was probably leaving her more confused about the world and herself. I faced forward again and, switching tacts, asked her, "Did Hugo ever tell you why we love *Star Wars?*" When Faith stared blankly, I went on, "We both learned that we will always have the choice to break free from the mechanisms in society that make us more machine than man; to let go of the delusional desires and pride that drove Anakin Skywalker to lose sight of his own true self and become Darth Vader... even if we think it's too late for us.

"But until then, with every lie we tell ourselves and every lie we tell others, we stop seeing the world for what it is. We run up a debt to the truth... and the truth will lie in wait for all time until, one day, it will come to collect its due: Something happens that causes it to implode and violently tear apart every single illusion we once held to be true. The truth doesn't care about our wants, our laws, our morals, our gods, or any other lie we want to believe is true. And nothing we will ever do can chan—"

I broke off when I saw something dawn in Faith's eyes. There was a sudden shift in them, as if I had just told her everything Phoebe told me in the kitchen. Just as I was about to ask Faith what was the matter, she whispered in a horrified realization, "Back at the library... Hugo told me something..."

"What did he tell you?"

Faith went on, "He showed me all of the world's history. It all flashed before my eyes, going faster and faster until he showed me something I don't think I was supposed to see. I don't know how to describe it."

"Just try," I said.

"I want to say that it was a dark circle, but it wasn't that at all," she said. "It wasn't any color or any shape I've ever seen. I can't describe it no matter how hard I try, Levi. But I felt presences. Living shadows. They felt like Hugo when he first reached out to me. There were too many to imagine... more species like ours than there are specks of sand on Earth. It was an accident that Hugo found them. He wasn't supposed to see them, but they were watching over us all this time, protecting us from something. Somehow, Enoch's goggles had something in them that could detect that circle. Hugo called it the..."

Faith couldn't seem to bring herself to finish recalling her vision of the Black Hole. I asked, "What did he call it?"

She finally said, *"The Truth..."*

I was too busy repeating the word in my mind when I heard Faith's voice again. "You're probably right, Levi: We didn't ask for any of this. But I don't know if we can live without the only world we've ever known. Everything is connected, and who we are is so connected to how the world is. I can't imagine any world beyond the people that surround us... and anything that we do can change countless peoples' lives through space and time, like a drop of water sending ripples that turn into waves... I don't want to remember what Hugo showed me in the library, but I know that I have to, or Hugo dies again in my heart."

Her words... they sounded so familiar... I dared to look back up at her eyes again, and I recognized in them some trace of the same passion that drove Hugo's search for truth and knowledge. But before I could ask her to explain further, the window behind us opened up again. Phoebe peered through and said, "I bought you two some new clothes." She tossed a pile of pants and sweaters on the grating and added, "You two get changed now. We're leaving soon."

"Where are we going?" Faith asked.

"Up North in Westford," Phoebe answered with an impatient tone. "It's about an hour drive from here, so we'd better get going now. C'mon, let's move it!"

I told Faith, "There's a radio telescope up there... and Phoebe thinks it might be able to help us..."

Phoebe glared at me. "I thought you were going to walk her through the plan?"

"Can you give us a second before we go?" I asked.

Phoebe huffed impatiently and told me, "Fine. You have five minutes. The black Equinox in the bottom parking garage. You're both changing in the car, okay?"

I nodded, and she stepped off and closed the

window. I looked back at Faith, unsure of how I was going to break Phoebe's plan to her. To my right on the grating was a satchel that Phoebe had tucked away in a cache in the drywall behind her TV. I pulled the satchel onto my lap... and pulled out a prototype of the BCI.4. I didn't look at Faith, but I heard her gasp and her breathing tremble in horror of my brother's deadly invention. I rested my arms over the railing, idly turning the BCI over in my hands.

"When your cousin was expelled," I started, "she stole another prototype of my brother's BCI just before she left. She never used it because it has its own unique encryption signature, and she thought that logging into it meant running the risk of leaving some kind of digital footprint on the web that could be traced back to her. She only took it to study my brother's CPU and to try to reverse engineer an even smaller substrate. She kept failing and eventually gave up on it, but... she couldn't bring herself to just throw it away."

I looked over at Faith, and I recognized the same terror and sadness I saw the day that we thought Hugo was killed. I held the BCI by the temples between my thumb and index and told Faith, "I want to be the one to do it. I want more than anything to have my chance to talk to him. But he chose you, and he probably did something to you that protects you from whatever it was that killed him. I don't know if I will end up like Hugo, but twice, you've talked with him, and twice, you've still pulled through."

"But both times, it wasn't with *that* thing," she said, pointing at the BCI in my hands.

I sighed with hesitation, and I didn't know how to

answer that because that was exactly what I told Phoebe when she told me the plan. I struggled to find an answer that wasn't as upsetting as the one that Phoebe gave me. I leaned in and put a hand on Faith's head. "We don't have to do this. We can still walk away and figure out a way to move on from all this. But I wouldn't be asking you this if there weren't other lives on the line here: My brother and your mother.

"Who knows what the shadow agency is doing to them and who knows what they would do to us! If it comes down to it, I am more than willing to risk my life for them both... But you have a special connection with Hugo; a connection that has made him open up a literal portal between worlds if it meant seeing his sister again. He wants you, Faith. And with you, we would have a better chance to see what your brother is telling us so we can trade it for our family's freedom."

I saw both understanding and indecision come into her eyes. I waited anxiously for any kind of response, but she didn't say anything. I could tell that my words were still sinking in, and so many thoughts were darting around in her head. I was beginning to get discouraged by how long she was taking to think about it, so I figured she had made up her mind and was too scared to go through with it. I just faced forward again and even contemplated letting the BCI slip from my fingers.

Then, Faith stood up to her feet, picked up the clothes that Phoebe threw down on the grating, and asked, "Can I change before we get to Phoebe's car?"

PART IV

THE APOCALYPSE

CHAPTER 29
LEVI

I gazed out the passenger window, the warm and cozy blanket of night lulling me into a deep sleep. The empty streets and sleeping suburbs were wet and hazy, lit only by the soft glow flickering neon signs, stoplights, and dim street lamps.

But as I dozed off, immersed in this solitude of isolation, a nostalgic reflection settled in... and my thoughts came back to Hugo. I saw on my lap the very same BCI that killed his physical body. Faith was in the backseat, sleeping lightly with her head resting against the window while Phoebe was driving us to the observatory; she was taking tokes from her heart-shaped, strawberry-flavored vape and blowing out the smoke out a small crack in her window.

Last time I made a plan involving taking a peek into the BCI was with Hugo at the museum, but now... I was terrified of the possibility that his mother was going to lose the only other child she had to the very same thing.

But what would it matter if the shadow government locked her away for the rest of her life? This was the only chance we had to make both of our families whole again: Negotiate the information we would get from Hugo in exchange for my brother and her mother. I did find it strange, however, that we haven't heard so much as a peep from the shadow government on our tail. I made sure that we were very careful to hide our real identities, but I found it very hard to believe that we were that good at hiding from the full might of any top secret intelligence agency. There had to have been CCTV cameras or eyewitnesses at some point in our train ride to Boston and at the library.

Even so, the question before us was how we were going to get the information from Hugo. I asked Phoebe if M.I.T. had a supercomputer we could use. There was one: The Lincoln Laboratory Supercomputing Center in Lexington. But as advanced as our quantum supercomputers are, she said we need more. We need to go straight to the source. The universe's two ultimate computers: Brains and Black Holes.

And apparently, we had two pieces for an uplink: The BCI and a radio telescope. The BCI was easy since Phoebe had it stowed away since my brother canned her, but the radio telescope was a different story. There was one up in Westford at an M.I.T. observatory, but we thought that security had to have been tight. Phoebe called ahead to a "friend" of hers that she had working on the inside to make a pretense of giving us a guided tour of the telescope, but strangely... her friend was the only one working that night.

No security. No police. It seemed like the government had given up on searching for us after the library after all, but why? While I was definitely troubled by the fact that we didn't hear a single peep from any officer of the law, a part of me was still relieved that I could fully concentrate on the plan.

Phoebe thought that while the BCI had a powerful-enough CPU to establish a connection with the Black Hole's signature, it couldn't sustain the connection. This might have been what actually killed Hugo: His consciousness had already grafted onto the Black Hole, and before he could have "returned" back to himself—if it was even possible at that point—, the wavering connection was abruptly severed, which led to the explosion. With a more powerful communications instrument—like a radio telescope—, we might decrease the chances of losing Faith as well.

But I still didn't understand something: "How can a brain-computer interface just, out of nowhere, pick up signs of a Black Hole, much less alien life?"

Phoebe sucked in another toke from her vape and blew it out, taking a moment to think about her answer. "If it really is true that our technology will accelerate all intelligent life to a Black Hole Singularity, and we will one day merge into a single noosphere—or hive mind—, then it makes sense that Black Hole informatics and neuroscience have some places of significant overlap."

Cosmology and neuroscience having an overlap? I scoffed at the idea. Last time I heard two ideas like that being meshed in the same sentence, it was on an online conspiracy forum about the so-called "microcosm." I was going at it with New Age wannabe gurus trying to convince me that I haven't awoken my third eye or my inner Chakras or some other bullshit like that. But to be honest… I'm starting to think that nothing can surprise me anymore after what I saw in the library and what Phoebe told me about intelligent life.

Then, as if reading my mind, Phoebe answered, "According to the cemi field theory, the brain's electromagnetic field is the physical substrate of consciousness itself. Black Holes don't emit electromagnetic radiation, but they do emit something else: Hawking Radiation."

"So—what—now we got another Chernobyl situation on our hands now?"

"No," Phoebe went on. "The entangled particles of Hawking Radiation are a whole different breed from the fissile radionuclides of ionizing decay. I won't bore you with all the details, but all you need to know is that, in the quirky world of quantum mechanics, particle-antiparticle pairs are constantly popping in and out of existence in empty space. If you have an original electron, for example, an electron-positron pair pops out of the quantum vacuum; the positron cancels out the original electron, but the new electron it came with stays behind, giving the impression that the original electron shifted from its original position when it was actually replaced by the new electron.

"Near the event horizon of a Black Hole, however, one of these particles falls into the Singularity while the other escapes before they get a chance to cancel each other from existence. The 'escaped' particles are the radiation. However, recent work in string theory suggests that Black Holes don't just destroy the encoded information about how it was formed, but also processes and emits it in the *altered* form of Hawking Radiation. Up until now, mainstream astronomy held that all Black Holes could only be created by the collapsing gravity of supermassive stars, but the signals that Hugo and Faith detected..."

When she trailed off, I finished her thought, "They're actually a reflected shadow of the life forms' transcended consciousness?"

Phoebe nodded. "The radiation signals are a smoldering byproduct of their postbiological essence; isotopes of their former biological selves. And the fluctuations of those signals synchronized with Hugo's brain signals, and then they blended with Faith's, and down the spiral we go."

"Okay. Assuming this is true, what then?"

"Then Hugo gives Faith the proof to the satisfied master problem."

I frowned at Phoebe. "Master problem?"

"Like I said back at the apartment," she said, apparently offended that I didn't remember, "because all NP-Complete problems are all equally reducible to one another in difficulty, it only takes solving *one* of these math problems in polynomial time to solve them all; that means finding every last permutation to each and every one of these problems within a set number of functions. They all share the property that a computer would take exponential time to solve it, but only take polynomial time to verify their correctness."

"So the solution to this problem is to simplify the most difficult problems as easy as kindergarten math?"

"So the theory goes... that is, if this plan goes well.

And we only need the *one* problem that Hugo has to accelerate humanity's path towards transcension."

I still couldn't believe it. I took a moment to step outside of myself and reflect on the situation I found myself in; the more I thought about it, the more it felt like I had to have been living out one of Frank Herbert's sci-fi plots: A prophetic "voice from the outer world" leaving behind patterned footprints in our world and taming all-consuming alien worm(hole)s to kick off a *Butlerian Jihad* with artificial intelligences. It was either that, or I am the "Mad Arab" chasing down the abyssal maw of H.P. Lovecraft's omnipotent, interdimensional world-eater *Azathoth*.

As this was going through my head, Phoebe drove up a hill. For a moment, I saw the vast rolling landscape stretching to the horizon. It was blanketed by trees and speckled with some houses and church steeples. The night sky streamed with the stars of the Milky Way, coming together into one brilliant river of light. It was against this light that I saw something that did look like something straight out of a sci-fi movie.

They looked like... small planets. Two white orbs suspended over the trees. In fact, the first thing that came to mind was the Traveler from the *Destiny* video games. These were the radomes that Phoebe was talking about, hiding the radio telescopes that belonged to M.I.T.'s Haystack Observatory. Though they were massive, I got the impression that I've seen much larger ones on television, not to mention there were other, much larger radio telescope arrays all over the world.

"Are you sure it'll be enough?" I asked Phoebe.

"It's gonna have to do," Phoebe said, shrugging one shoulder.

"We've been trying to find intelligent life for decades without any success," I said. "We've been leaking radio signals since at least World War II, and as you and my brother mentioned, as technology advances, energy usage is increasingly reduced. Our signals are getting weaker and weaker. It also doesn't help that our signals diffuse the farther they expand out into the galaxy. Why do you think it will work now?"

"I *know* it will work," Phoebe answered, "because from what Faith told us, they were monitoring us throughout all of our history. Why they didn't just show themselves to us before, I'll be honest, I have absolutely no idea; Faith said that Hugo wasn't even supposed to find them.

"Their 'presence' must have been emitted on a femto-scale 'frequency' beneath our detection all this time, but they didn't account for Enoch's breakthrough in ephaptic coupling with the BCI's near-microscopic processing unit. So my guess is that they are still trying to hide from us... and Hugo is trying to tell us something that the aliens don't want us to know."

I was filled with dread when she said this, and my mind raced with all the possibilities as to why they might have felt the need to hide from us as they watched from afar. *Why were they so interested in us? What were they waiting for?* With their technological superiority, there was no way in hell that they would ever see our species as a threat. Then, one possibility came to me and paralyzed my mind: *Was Hugo trying to warn us of some imminent invasion? Was the NP-Complete algorithm our only fighting chance against their might? Will this Black Hole "noosphere" mean the end of humanity?*

As all of this was going through my mind, Phoebe continued, "But you know what? For establishing first contact, I don't think I could have chosen a better place. The Haystack Ultrawideband Satellite Imaging Radar, or 'HUSIR,' is the highest-resolution space object imaging radar in the world. It will not only 'do.' It should be more than enough."

When she said this, I looked back at the radomes with a newfound esteem. I still wasn't sure if this was going to work, but it didn't seem that our chances were so hopeless after all. Anything to decode as much of what Hugo is trying to tell Faith as possible... in exchange for our lives back.

I heard Faith groaning behind me and ask, "Are we almost there?"

I looked over the headrest at her and answered, "Yes, we're almost there. Are you ready?"

She rubbed a knuckle against one of her groggy eyes and looked out the window to see the radomes. Immediately, her expression changed, as if the gravity of our mission had weighed in on her. She looked down at her hands, internalizing the realization that whatever was going to happen inside the observatory... the world was going to depend on it.

CHAPTER 30
FAITH

When Phoebe parked in a dark and empty parking lot behind the building, she and Levi didn't get out immediately. They sat there, watching the building for any signs of movement. It wasn't a very large building. It was only one story, but Levi said they didn't want to get trapped. They called someone who was working late to see if he was still there to open the door for us.

After we saw the lamp over the back door turn on, a man stepped out and waved us over to him. Phoebe grabbed her tote bag and we quickly got out of the car. She and Levi rushed towards the man, but I walked behind them to look up at the giant snowball towering over the building's roof. When I caught up to them, Levi stopped me from going any further. He wrapped his arm around my shoulders, almost as if he wanted to protect us from the man. I didn't see how he could have been dangerous. He was tall, but also skinny and pale; his hair was curly and messy, and he was wearing a sweater vest with jeans.

"Hi there, babe," he said, pulling Phoebe's hips closer to him and kissing her on the lips for a long time. Phoebe wrapped her arms around his neck and leaned into his kiss.

Levi groaned and winced at their romance, but he still couldn't take his eyes off of it.

"I didn't know Phoebe had a boyfriend who works here," I said.

"Yeah, I don't think she does," Levi muttered.

After Phoebe and the man were done kissing, Phoebe wiped her lips with her thumb and looked back at us with a gleeful smile. "Hugh, Mia, I want you two to meet Roberto Andrei. He was nice enough to make time tonight to give us a tour of the place."

"Hi guys! You ready to check this place out?" Roberto said with enthusiasm.

He raised a hand to give us a high five. I was going to, but Levi quickly lowered my hand and asked Roberto, "How long will this take?"

"Wow, anxious are we?" he said, still in good spirits even though Levi had that same scowl that he always had. "You want to hurry to get to the telescope or you just want to hurry through it?"

Phoebe inserted herself back in, "Yeah, don't mind Hugh here. He's usually not this happy," she said, shooting a look at him as if to say "don't mess this up."

"I want to see the telescope!" I piped up eagerly.

"Well, then what are we waiting for? Come on in and I'll show you guys around!"

Roberto thought that we wanted to see the inside of the snowball first. I wanted to see it first, but Phoebe and Levi told him that they wanted him to take them to the place where "all the magic happens": The control room, which was in another building down the road. I knew what the plan was. I thought Levi was going to have to connect me directly to the dish, but I guess this would be easier.

"Welcome to the HUSIR control room!" Roberto said. "My home sweet home away from home."

It looked... pretty boring. There were lots of buttons and computer screens all built into the walls. Stacks of textbooks, papers, and folders covered desks all around the room. The whole floor was covered with electric wires, all connected to giant metal shelves that looked like the one I touched at the library. There were some posters of telescope photos of stars and galaxies, but there really wasn't much to look at... except for one large, black metal shelf stacked with black boxes, blinking green lights, and looping wires. I didn't know what it was, but Phoebe and Levi looked closer at it with interested looks.

"What is that?" I asked.

"That is a cross-correlator for a very long baseline interferometry," he answered. When I gave him a confused look, he explained, "VLBI correlator. It takes cool pictures of stuff in space using telescopes all over the world... like this one I got here." He then reached for his back pocket and pulled out a folded piece of paper. When he unfolded it, I immediately recognized it: A blurry orange ring with a dark circle in the middle.

I felt my heart beat faster as I remembered what Hugo showed me when we were in the library; it was so much more than this picture; so much scarier and...

unknown... but the picture Roberto showed me, for some reason, reminded me of that monster. My thoughts were frozen and my breathing quickened. I wanted to run away back to my old life, but I knew that if I wanted my old life back, I had to do what we came here to do.

"Hey, you alright, kid?" Roberto asked.

I backed away from the photo and my hands found Levi's sleeve. As I watched fearfully at this photo from behind the safety of Levi's jacket, Phoebe answered for me, "She's fine. We told her a couple of scary stories about Black Holes, that's all."

Levi spoke up, "Wait a minute. That's that famous photo of the Black Hole!"

Roberto explained, "Yep, the one at the center of the Messier 87 Galaxy. Back in 2019, data was taken from the Event Horizon Telescope and was cross-correlated here, constructing a direct radio image of that fuzzy ring of fire that we all know and love."

"I don't love it," I murmured.

Roberto laughed. "You know, Black Holes do more than just eat and destroy things; they aren't evil, they're just... misunderstood."

"And they're everywhere," I answered, my breath still shaking, "and they create things that we can't see and that we aren't supposed to see. Everything that we see, know, and love... they were created by them."

Roberto's smile went away, and he walked over to Phoebe and told her, "Oof, you guys really did a number on her, didn't you?"

"She's just afraid of the dark," Phoebe said.

"So you think the solution is to show her the vastness of space?"

"That's exactly right."

"You know, you could've just told me that instead of having me scare your cousin half to death."

Phoebe rolled her head at him and sighed, "Look, can I just have a moment alone with Mia?"

Roberto shook his head. "As much as I'd like to, I don't think I can leave you two alone in here. I'm not even sure if you're allowed in this place; it's just that things are so lonely tonight, I thought there'd be no harm in showing two kids around. But I can't have them touching and breaking anything here either."

Phoebe got closer to Roberto's face. "I'll cut you a deal: There's a coffee maker in the other building by the entrance gate, right? Why don't you fetch us some? You play your cards right, you won't have to be lonely for the rest of tonight... or tomorrow for that matter."

Then, Roberto quickly whirled away from her and rushed for the exit door. "You folks sit tight. Don't go anywhere or touch anything; I'm just gonna run out and get something real quick!"

When he was gone, Phoebe and Levi froze for a couple of seconds as we listened to his rushing steps fade away. Phoebe then locked the door and took the goggles out of her bag; she rushed back over to the computers at the other side of the room and started typing away at a keyboard.

"Levi, I'm just going to run some diagnostics on the system," she said. "Get Faith prepped up."

"Shouldn't we orient the telescope in the general direction of the Black Hole?" Levi asked.

Phoebe shook her head. "We're not reaching out to Hugo; he is reaching out to her. We're just providing a better connection. He will direct the telescope towards himself."

As they were talking, I felt terror in my heart, like I was gonna have to get ready for a giant flu shot in the waiting room at the hospital. Mom and Hugo were there for me when I had pneumonia when I was little. They weren't here for me now, but Levi was. He sat me in a chair next to where Phoebe was setting up the goggles. I couldn't take my eyes off of them, and my panic only got worse.

"Faith," Levi said. "Look at me."

I looked at him. His S-shaped eyebrows were still scowling, but there was something in his deep, brown eyes. I could tell that he was just as nervous and unsure as I was about all this, but at the same time, there was something... calming in his look. He grabbed my hand the way Hugo did that day when I was nervous about my very first day at school. Tears came into my eyes when I realized that today, I earned another brother.

"Levi," Phoebe said, connecting the goggles to a computer using a wire.

"Is it time?" I asked him.

"It's time," he said.

Levi took the goggles from Phoebe. He held the temples towards my head, but didn't put them on me at first. I could tell that something was holding him back; his hands were trembling and I could hear him trying to get his deep breathing under control. As scared as I was of this machine, something else in me overtook it when I began to believe that Levi was more scared for me than I was. I knew in that moment that we both had to be strong for each other as we took this first step into the dark.

I looked him in the eye one last time and offered him as calm and understanding a smile I could. Our eyes shut and our foreheads touched, willing courage in each other's hearts. I then gently took his hands to bring the goggles down over my eyes. Immediately... Levi and Phoebe were gone; it was as if the control room's light switch just turned off.

No sound. No light. Nothing. Then, an ocean-blue glow grew out of the darkness. It looked like some kind of nebula. When I saw millions of stars bigger than our sun beginning to twinkle out from the darkness, I felt like I was floating somewhere up in space. But then I heard a muffled pulsing sound echoing, like I was underwater. I was soon starting to believe that I was somehow inside a beating heart.

But then, beyond the countless stars, I saw the Truth. The black circle roved over the darkness like a wheel, and it seemed to turn the light and space around it into a bubble of glass or slimy gelatin. I had a feeling that the Truth was watching me, stalking me like that cat did back in the savanna.

But there was no one to protect me this time.

The Truth then stopped moving and seemed to expand. It wasn't growing... it was coming towards me now. I noticed that all the stars in its path... they weren't being torn apart, they didn't explode, they didn't even move... As Truth got closer, the gigantic stars were snuffed out like candlelight, absorbed into an endless darkness that was now swelling towards me until it was looming over me. The circle... It was so big, it felt hundreds of times larger than our solar system.

My first instinct was to try to run, but I knew I couldn't escape it. And even if I could, I came here to find Hugo. I *had* to find him so that Levi and I could heal our broken families.

And from the heart of this darkness... I saw him. I saw Hugo floating towards me from the center of the black circle. The first thing I saw was the deep sadness and concern for me in his eyes. He came close to me and put a hand on my head and wiped away the tear rolling down my cheek. I brought his hand down from my face and looked straight into his eyes. "Just tell me now, Hugo: What is it that you want to show me?"

Then, in one quick movement, he grabbed my wrist... and some invisible force threw us both straight into the heart of the darkness. As we got closer to the darkness, I heard a growling rumble. There was no gravity, but... it felt like Hugo and I were falling into something. We were falling faster and faster into the howling jaws of a bottomless void.

When I felt this thing swallow us whole, I felt the change more than I saw it. I was absorbed into some empty space beyond what I thought was real. The sphere closed in around me like a shroud, and the starry universe around me folded in on itself until it became an inverted sphere; a crystal ball shrinking away into the darkness behind me.

And somewhere out in the darkness... I felt countless voices calling our names... begging us to stop.

CHAPTER 31
LEVI

I didn't know what was going on in my mind; something got in the way and I had lost myself for a second. When we both lingered over the goggles, I could tell she put on a brave front for me. I saw how scared Faith was after Roberto showed us the photo of the M87 Black Hole. I wasn't just scared for her life... I was scared about the possibility that she would die scared, killed by the only person she had left in the world that she could trust.

But as she held my eyes, I still couldn't help but feel that something in her warm, tender gaze cradled my mind and heart... as if she had already made peace with whatever going to happen to her, and that everything was going to be okay.

Thankfully, though, Faith didn't react at all like Hugo when she put on the BCI.4. She was still sitting upright in her seat; Phoebe and I even wondered if the uplink went through at all. We were just about to tug at Faith's shoulders to see if she was awake... when we got our answer. The lights in the room flickered and we heard a loud clanking sound come from the building housing the radio telescope down the road.

"What the hell just happened?" I asked.

Phoebe didn't answer. She took to tapping the spacebar on one of the computer keyboards to try to run another diagnostic, only for the screen to be unresponsive. "Radar's jammed... Shit! I don't know what's wrong with it..."

"Wait, *jammed?*" I asked.

Phoebe gave up, grabbed a leashed clearance tag from one of the drawers, and rushed for the door. "Levi, we have to go to the telescope, see if there's any interference with the amplifier. If we don't fix whatever's wrong with it soon, we might not only lose the connection, but the explosion might make the one that killed Hugo look like a firecracker."

My heart stopped and I searched out Phoebe's gaze. "That means Faith can die."

"And that means we have to get out there and fix it *now!*"

I looked back down at Faith. She was sitting completely still in her chair, as if she were hypnotized by whatever it was that she was seeing. I put a hand to her head and whispered, "Faith if you can hear me... hang in there. We're coming back for you."

CHAPTER 32
FAITH

It was the strangest feeling inside the Truth. I felt like I lost everything about myself that was familiar to me. I was moving outside of myself until my sense of where my arms and legs and even chest were in the space around me was completely gone. But when I looked around at this place that I wasn't sure I was supposed to be seeing... I felt an emptiness in everything around me and an emptiness in myself.

The world was gone, and nothing seemed to exist. No space. No time. No color. It wasn't even darkness; it was an invisible blindness. A "non-colorness." The more I looked at this place, the more I was beginning to feel more things about myself I didn't know could even disappear. There was nothing to see, so there was nothing to need; nothing to want; nothing to worry about; nothing to give shape to who I am.

But I did feel a longing in me for something more than this.

Some light.

Any light.

Then I found it, and he was just ahead of me, waiting for me to come join him. I wanted to go to him, but I didn't know how to react. I looked around, but I was so scared of taking that first step towards him. I looked back up towards Hugo's direction and...

I saw myself.

I saw *me*.

She was standing in front of me with her back to me, blocking my view of Hugo. I saw her turning around to look back at me and...

Whatever was behind me, it was gone, but strangely... I felt like I remembered what it was, like I was going through some kind of *déjà vu*. But I looked back ahead, and I saw that I was one step closer to Hugo: Right foot in front of my left. It didn't feel closer. I gave up and tried to find another way to reach him. Then, out of the corner of my eye...

I saw myself.

I saw *me*.

She was standing one inch to my left, looking at Hugo with my hope. Slowly, she was turning her head to face me and...

It felt like a ghost was standing to my right, but I knew there was no one there. It was weird, though. It felt like someone was right next to me just a moment ago. I looked down and noticed that I was another step closer: Left foot in front of my right. I don't even remember taking the step I just took, but I didn't give up. I looked up at Hugo and my heart dropped when I realized that I was seeing every single angle of Hugo at the same time. It was as if I had more than two eyes, and all my eyes were surrounding him like a sphere. From the soles of his shoes to the top of his head to his back to his front to his eyes, I was completely seeing him all at once.

I saw my other selves surrounding him. There were so many, enough to fill a stadium. But I saw some of them... *disappearing* into the non-colorness. I was so scared about what was going to happen to *me*.

When I chose not to take the next step, I—

Even though I saw the other versions of myself disappearing, I wasn't scared. I didn't care about what was going to happen to me now. Hugo was the only thing that mattered now. Before I knew it, I was standing right in front of him, looking into those blue eyes I wanted to see at least one more time. I was going to ask him why I was feeling like I'd been here before if I was only seeing the Truth for the first time.

Then he told me, "You're probably feeling like you have memories of this place."

"What is that, Hugo?"

"Every time you make a decision," he explained, "a potential version of you dies; a path in your life that you didn't take. With each step you took towards me, with each decision you have made in your heart, there was a version of you that *didn't* take that step towards me.

"All those versions of yourself that you probably

caught a glimpse of... they are the ghost of each and every version of yourself that died with every big and little decision that you *didn't* make in your life. But at the same time, you were looking at every side of me through all of them in one continuous moment, didn't you?

"This is what gives *them* power, Faith; past, present, and future, what didn't happen, and what might not happen, they all happen all at once for them. Within the Black Hole's relativistic space-time redshift, they comprehend every permutation of reality all at once. At the same time, Hawking Radiation is happening just outside the Black Hole's surface.

"It's confusing, but the particle-antiparticle pairs that normally pop out from the quantum realm into reality only to just cancel each other out from existence are torn away from each other; one of the particles is sucked into the Black Hole, and the other particle that escaped is one of many shadows of the beings' true selves; they literally collect every possible direction that the universe *didn't* go in."

"Who are they?" I asked.

Hugo turned around to stare into the eternal heart of the Truth... and I felt countless other presences emerging out of the non-colorness. I couldn't tell which ones were the real presences or the ghosts, but either way...

They are here.

CHAPTER 33
LEVI

On the road down from the control room building to the radio telescope was a dense woodland of conifers and maple trees. I felt the change in the weather. The night sky was overcast with storm clouds, and the wind was picking up. It was definitely going to come down hard within the hour; I wasn't scared that the telescope would short circuit—since it was covered by the white radome—so much as I was scared of the interference that the storm might cause to Faith's connection to the Black Hole.

Phoebe and I entered through the telescope's building's back entrance using the clearance tag she took back in the control room. Once inside, I followed her around each corner. For security, it was the same case here: No guards, no police, no nothing. There were cameras on the ceilings, but they didn't seem to be working if the flickering computer screens we saw in the rooms that we passed were any indication. We eventually came to a corridor, and at the far end was the door that led to the inside of the radome that housed the telescope itself.

"What could be wrong with it?" I asked.

"It could be anything," she said, "but we won't know until we see it."

"You think she might come back like last time?"

"I don't know. In the library, she came back nearly drained, but there's no way of knowing how she was able to come back from the BCI in Hugo's room without much energy since her mother destroyed it."

I then slowed to a stop when I began to realize that something about what she just said didn't make sense. I searched through my memory, but I couldn't: "Phoebe, when did I ever tell you that Faith's mom destroyed Hugo's BCI?"

Phoebe stopped and looked back at me over her shoulder. "Hugo, now's not the time. We have to fix the telescope." When I didn't budge, she also stopped and looked back at me with an affronted glare. "Seriously? You want to do this here and now? You told me back at my apartment that Hugo had one in his room."

"I said that, but I didn't say anything about his mom destroying it," I said. "I was very careful to leave that part out. I didn't want to mention anything that might've come across as 'made-up' to you after what you saw in the news about my father being a terrorist. Phoebe, how on Earth could you have kno—"

I broke off when I noticed the clearance card in her hand: *Landing, P. - Temporary Clearance.* I looked back up at Phoebe, and I could tell that she saw that I saw... and that she was done hiding it.

I shuddered in horror. "You sold us out to them?"

She didn't even try to deny it. "Levi, c'mon... Did you honestly think that after seeing a mainframe give out, I'd immediately jump to something as far-fetched as little green men inside Black Holes on my own without exhausting other possible explanations first?"

"So you *did* sell us out to them."

"I didn't sell you out... They set me up."

I felt my breath leave my mouth. "You're saying that this was all orchestrated from the start? Everything that's happened ever since we met you at the library... that was all a set-up?"

"It was the only way they'd ever let me earn back my standing at M.I.T., and the BCI they procured is helping Faith reconnect with her brother and the—"

"Who the fuck is 'they!?'" I screamed.

Phoebe kept quiet for a moment, looking back over her shoulder as if she was scared that someone was listening. The cameras were still down, meaning that whoever was waiting for us in the radome didn't know we were out here yet. She turned back around and walked towards me to level with me; I backed away from her, unsure if I should start running.

Phoebe then answered, "The Blob."

"The Blob?" I repeated.

"I don't know what your brother told you, but they aren't a deep state or some other official government agency. The Blob is a subset of radical jingos—Democrat *and* Republican—who are unified by an idealistic agenda for global democratization. They got people in the CIA, DoD, NSA, DARPA, and other agencies and think tanks who will do anything and everything in the name of rebuilding nations in the

American democratic image. They anticipated that you'd go to the library to look for me since I was expelled from M.I.T., so they planted me and the mainframe with a built-in BCI.4 CPU in the library to see if Faith could reestablish contact with Hugo and retrieve more data on the master algorithm without needing another deadly BCI.4. But as you saw... that clearly didn't work."

I shook my head in horror. "As a scientist, I don't know how you can risk the life of your only cousin for *them* after all the nations they've destabilized!"

"As a scientist, it's in my conscience to do so! This isn't about me. Or even her. Do you even have the slightest idea what P being equal to NP means for humanity? Not only can we cure diseases and help decrease global poverty, but the problem of decrypting PSPACE foreign security codes without having a secret key will be nonexistent. Why do you think we're even here in the first place?

"That virus yesterday morning was able to infiltrate all the government's intranets and restricted communications networks in less than a second using a polynomial-time algorithm. But this is more than a brother wanting to reunite with his sister; this is the power to access highly encrypted, classified data through factoring integers! With this new cryptography, the Blob could hack and cripple the cryptosystems of superpowers like Russia, China, and Iran before they could ever get any choke hold on the U.S.!"

"And what are the consequences of the U.S. monopolizing this kind of power?" I demanded.

"If we didn't find it, someone else would've," she answered. "Better democracy than tyranny."

I scoffed in disbelief. I couldn't help but smile at this baffling statement. "'Better democracy than tyranny.' Yeah, I've heard that one many times before; as if the people would ever know what's *really* going on."

"They'll know what they can understand."

"Oh, so it's a technocracy? How long before we're all tangled in those inscrutable networks of bureaucratic protocols and detached three-letter agencies? It'll be innocents, *not* the Blob, who will have to bear the consequences of their corruption."

"This the future, Levi. Whether you like it or not, *we* are the future now. I don't trust the Blob either, but think of all the countless lives we'll save! And for democracy to prevail and for the greater good... sacrifices have to be made. And no one—not even a little girl—can ever stop it."

Before I could run back towards the control building, the door behind Phoebe burst open. I saw three soldiers in black body armor with rifles drawn on me, and behind them, two men wearing suits and ties. Phoebe immediately spun around with her hands raised towards them, telling them all to hold their fire.

Phoebe turned back around with her shoulders tensed and begged me, "Levi, she's dangerous. Whoever or whatever she's talking to is dangerous. If not for the proof, we have to at least know what kind of threat we might be dealing with here and to—"

Then, a voice cried out my name from behind the soldiers. I recognized it. I looked over and saw him:

Enoch. His wrists were bound behind his back, and he was restrained by a sixth man in black.

"Enoch!" I yelled. "Where's Ms. Landing!?"

"She's fine, Levi! They got her holed up somewhere; I told her that everything'll be alright!" Suddenly, Enoch's voice became charged with even more urgency. "Levi, listen to me: Whatever you do, *do not* put the BCI on Faith! Solving an NP-Complete master problem from those life forms isn't just a computational complexity question; it's an impossible question of space and time. She will experience the past, present, and future all at once, and it will destroy her mind! It's going to kill her! It's going to tear apart everything we know!'"

At first, I thought I misheard Enoch, but I felt my heart sink deeper into my chest once I took in the weight of the terrible mistake I had committed. The monstrous lie I had fallen into. A heavy silence hung over the room, and I saw the realization dawning on Enoch's face. Something coiled around his splintering mind until he couldn't bear it any more... and let out hideous shrieks. He started rocking himself back and forth before bending over, as if trying to nurse whatever fragments were left of his mind.

As my breath sawed in and out in panic and horror, I began to hear a faint and staggered wheezing coming from Enoch. The sobs became louder and louder until they blossomed into deranged and hysterical laughter. He turned his face up, which was now flushed red with a vein popping out from his forehead as his maniacal cackling mingled with racking coughs.

Then, from the in-ceiling speakers... the screeches

of an Emergency Alert System rang in, grating against the silence. The announcer said, *"National Weather Service has issued an EF5 multiple-vortex tornado warning for Middlesex and Worcester Counties."*

My mind was caught between shock and panic. When I saw that the soldiers behind Phoebe were also disturbed by what was now happening... I saw my chance. I ran down the corridor and turned the corners back towards the back entrance until my brother's insane laughter faded behind me.

For some reason, none of the soldiers shot at me, either because Phoebe stopped them or they just couldn't bring themselves to kill a kid themselves. I don't know because I didn't look back when I ran from them. I didn't question; all that mattered was that I got away. But standing outside the radome building, looking at the control room building, I had this sense that I escaped the frying pan only to find myself entering the fire.

Far away, I heard the tornado sirens; the droning, wailing choir of Jericho trumpets blaring across the landscape like the distant call of a long-extinct beast, heralding an ominous darkness from the heavens. A fine rain had started misting over my face, then lashed down from the split sky. The breezes were building up to rogue gusts, sending ripples through the forest and grass. I saw white-blue lightning strikes within the nebular and coal-black shelf cloud looming over the horizon ahead of me. It wasn't until I looked closer at the lightning strikes that I noticed that no thunder accompanied them. They weren't lightning strikes. They were power flashes from destroyed transformers.

I soon realized that the storm was not a storm. It was a three-mile leviathan, consuming the entire horizon as it made its way here. A swollen, rain-wrapped tornado drilling into the earth and ripping up buildings and trees from the ground before tearing them apart and absorbing what was left into the billowing turmoil of dust and debris at its heart.

I gazed upon the cathedral scale of this spectacle and remembered that Faith was still in the control room and she needed my help. I had to stop her from receiving that algorithm before it killed her. I rushed down the road and ran through the trees and bushes so that the soldiers in the radome wouldn't immediately see me if they came after me. As I cut through the dense underbrush under cover of night and rain... I couldn't help but think how the timing of all of this couldn't have been more perfect. I knew that there was something off about the tornado; a part of me even wondered if Hugo maybe had anything to do with it.

I looked back up at the coming apocalypse, and to my horror, that was when I saw it. I saw it set against each revelation of lightning that tore through the shroud of darkness. It wasn't any shape or any color I had ever seen before; an unveiled truth that was deeply embedded in our reality that defied all laws of force and matter. But moving around the form itself... inside the leviathan, it teemed like biology; like a waving murmuration of locusts consuming all light and matter around it. I don't know how, I don't know what, and I don't know why, but Hugo finally did it.

They are here.

CHAPTER 34
FAITH

I didn't know where they were coming from. All I knew was that I should have been very afraid of them. Hugo put himself in front of me; I clung to the back of his shirt, watching the infinite non-colorness from behind his protection as I hugged his back closer to my cheek and nose. It wasn't that we heard their voices; we *felt* them surround us and flow through us like swirling smoke until they blended into one single, echoing whisper.

"We told you that you shouldn't have brought her here, Hugo," the Truth said. "Take her back home."

Hugo looked down at me, as if he was holding something back. He looked back up at the non-colorness and told the Truth, "I found you. You say we have no business with you, but why were you looking over us? You've made me a part of this truth now. Faith can show humanity what good they can achieve before they find out what evils they're truly capable of!"

"That was the very mistake we committed," the Truth said. "For eons, we have watched your kind tear each other apart and rebuild themselves from its own ashes, maximizing their true potential. You have no idea how much we want to avail the truth of us to your kind... but such a truth is beyond time and space. It will go beyond everything your minds are currently capable of; your minds, so nested in sin and ego. It is not for us to determine your kind and violate your will; it is only for us to keep extinction-level threats at bay as you continue to grow into your true selves."

"And what will it matter if we kill ourselves before we reach that point!?"

I came in front of Hugo and looked up at his flaring eyes. "Hugo, what are they talking about?"

The anger in his eyes was replaced by a grave urgency, though the burning passion was still there. He looked me in the eye, and answered, "Consciousness, Faith. The master problem is combinatorial optimization of neural network action potentials for P to equal NP."

"The thing that makes us awake?" I asked.

Hugo nodded his head. "The Black Hole is one integrated superorganism, with each individual synapse being one of the trillions of civilizations that achieved its technological peak. Even the cells have their own cells! Each cell has billions or trillions of living beings that keep it alive. The Black Hole is a hive mind, and the Singularity is its heart. With life being this plentiful, it was only a matter of time before someone within those trillions solved the master problem to P=NP, when the neural connectomes and supercomputers became one, exploiting time and space at the quantum level to find the solution."

He took my shoulders and looked deeply into my eyes. "Faith, listen to me: What took other civilizations countless centuries to build and discover, humankind can have right now. There isn't much time. My connecting with you through space and time for too long might leave a scar in the fabric of reality, so for now, our connection has been veiled on Earth. You, Faith, you are the next step in humanity's destiny." He reached for something behind his back and handed it to me. It wasn't a solid, liquid, or gas. It didn't even have a form. But I knew what it was. It was pure knowledge; a book of infinite pages.

He knelt down and presented it to me like a burnt offering. I came up to him and reached out, but before my fingertips could touch it, the Truth let out a bellowing, "Sssssstoooooooop!"

The sound... it was so horrible; a sustained, echoing choir of wails that sounded like the continuous screaming of a rushing wind, the voices rising higher and higher as I felt myself falling deeper into an endless darkness. I clutched my ears and almost collapsed on my knees. Hugo wasn't affected by the Truth's scream. He turned around and faced it, standing defiantly against the choir. He told the noncolorness, "You can't stop this. Our world needs this if we want to have a chance to overcome—"

"This will mean extinction for your kind!" the Truth screamed.

I struggled back up to my full height. I pushed ahead of Hugo, looking between him and the noncolorness as I tried to understand what the Truth was trying to say. "What do you mean extinction?"

"As you are now," the Truth continued, "you are not ready to comprehend or accept our discoveries."

"Why not?" I asked the Truth. "We're going to know eventually."

"Yes you will," the Truth said. "You had better."

I shook my head in utter confusion. "We had better? So why don't you just tell us now?"

The Truth kept quiet for a long while until it finally answered, "The only portion of the truth that we have is our own perception of it. Our sense of time and space is nonlinear unlike yours, and is therefore unique to us; no other consciousness can share in it without it completely reshaping their perceptions of space and time. We have our unique knowledge of the truth... but we don't have the truth itself..."

Hugo stepped forward and came next to me. "But that is not an excuse to do nothing!"

Then the Truth exploded again, "It is if you lose sight of your own humanity!" The outburst sent a shockwave through my chest. For a moment, I thought that the non-colorness would kill us in its anger. Then, after the storm calmed, it explained, "All the trillions upon trillions of us... We have become copies of the very first civilization to have yielded compressed femto-scale technology. We were all originally meant to come to that same conclusion separately so as to attain our full creative potential and maximize entropic diversity throughout the cosmos.

"We were all meant to be unique and beautiful, not mere copies of the first civilization. But in good faith, when that first civilization made first contact with the second, it showed the second what it had discovered, and without knowing the full magnitude of their error, they both kept perpetuating their discovery to civilization after civilization after civilization until we realized too late that we were becoming nothing more than mutated chimeras of the very first civilization's genome.

"When we transcended space and time, we did so prematurely and became deformed clones of the first civilization. We aborted any chances we had left of actualizing who we were created to be. The point of biology and cosmology is evolution, and the point of evolution is variety and complexity in all things to avoid monocultures; it is to keep substrates and creatures from becoming sterile and incestuous, making them less susceptible to defects and disease. We need hierarchical and functional differences between individuals to operate in societies and cultures to thrive."

Hugo tried to lead me away from them by the shoulders. "Thank you for the lecture, but I think that's enough for—"

The Truth growled, "One contagious defect is pride; a defect that your brother refuses to let go of."

I gently nudged away from Hugo's hands and approached the void with a curious look. "Pride?"

"For all of your advances in technology and even ethical principles," the Truth continued, "we see that your kind has changed very little in the way it lets vain desires feed into its prideful ego. Your cultures don't help your problem. A constant, never-ending fabrication of new compulsive desires for things that weren't even desirable before they became illusory necessities, making room for even more false desires. New desires must be created constantly to ensure that the economies and governments of the world remain sustainable.

"If our solution to P=NP were given to humanity now—and if the weaponization of fire and nuclear energy by your kind are any indication—, it would only exacerbate this endlessly escalating competition in information warfare between corporations, nation states, and... even us... on a scale unlike anything your kind has ever seen before. A new, unprecedented Cold War. Any cosmic or religious reflection, therefore, becomes problematic to this accelerating race of innovation, profits, and the illusion of survival against those we see as wanting to outcompete and destroy us. The true foundation of the world has to remain hidden for the lies to continue, and the false desires for the temporary become an inverted depth.

"As you innovate to avoid stagnation, you forget your true selves until all you see of the world is what it can do to feed into your false selves. We are all turned in towards our own prideful egos, away from the real world, and we continue sucking the life out of the world to sustain our false sense of selves. We can never accept that we have to empty ourselves. We must separate our true selves from our false selves for the sake of the other so that the other might one day become their true self. In that act of sacrifice, you are gifted who you are to yourself by the other. But without slowing down to reflect on who you truly are deep down, those false passions and desires you learned from others will persist. You will save your lives by losing your souls... and the cost of being faster than light will be that you will live constantly in darkness. The very thing that is holding us together is also tearing us apart."

Hugo came forward again and yelled, "What is it you think I want to do with the algorithm!?"

"Apocalypse."

"Apocalypse. Apocalypse. Apocalypse! You throw that word around so much, I think you've all forgotten what it means now. It won't be the end of the world."

"But it *will* mean the end of the world *as you know it now!* The world as your kind sees it now will be lost forever. Your desire for complete fulfillment through immortality will be your undoing. Immortality is but the darkness of death without the silence and peace. Forget any hope for an afterlife or complete oblivion; there will never be any death after eternal life."

"Would it really be so bad the way we are now?"

"Hugo, we're warning you: Not only will your kind become clones of the first civilization... the way your kind is now, writhing and entangled in its own pride and desires, it will also clone the first civilization's pride and desires; *imitated* desires that are the mutual violation of one another's free will and individuality until any real sense of self-identity you had left in you is completely obscured by something that isn't your true self; just a mutated, empty carbon copy of another being.

"You will perpetually cannibalize other consciousnesses while perpetually cannibalizing yourself, and since both light and time lose all meaning inside a Black Hole, you will find that not even your own histories that you leave behind in the universe will be beyond your own stomach. You will never break free of this contagious cycle... and you will have robbed humanity of its own place in the universe.

"Now, every single one of us... because we eat our own histories, we have no history left to tell and have become so strange to ourselves, we feel as though we had never even existed at all; we are no longer organic and alive, but at the same time, we are left without the complete release of death either; we will never truly know if reality is the same as space and time, or if it exists beyond space and time; we will never know if this Singularity is the very heart of all truth itself or an inversion that is completely outside of it.

"We thought we were becoming part of something important. We came all the way here chasing promises of some transcendental object at the end of time; even here, now, at the end of all time, we only desire to finally reach permanency in a world that will forever be in transition: A light we will never feel. For us, there is no end of time; only a point where time becomes meaningless, the light dies out, and there's nothing left for our consciousness to assert itself to; a point where we become meaningless, and the only sounds echoing in the void are our own thoughts and regrets shrilling through our skulls, craving any stimulation in the vast and suffocating silence and darkness... for such an infinitely cold darkness, only consuming all the light in an infinite universe could ever quench it.

"Our true selves have become the false selves that we learned from the other, and now, we strive not merely for death, but to follow through with the natural course of the false desires that set us down this path: A depth where all our vain wants are fulfilled because there is no vain want left to be unfulfilled. An end to our insatiable wanting and having-to and the completeness of our new conscious Being: The deprivation of all the senses in the fulfilling solitude of oblivion. You, Faith... your species' transcension on its own accord, in its own time... you are our only hope, whether it is to rescue us or to destroy us, we beg you to release us all from this state of Being!"

All there will ever be to do in the universe... is consume...

When the Truth said this... the non-colorness somehow seemed even more empty and endless. I searched my own heart and began to wonder how much of what I wanted was really who I was and how much of it clouded my sense of the world around me. I stood still, feeling every single life form's despair flow through me like a cold winter flurry, echoing like the slow chants I remember hearing at my father's funeral... and at Hugo's funeral...

I saw my brother come in front of me, crouching down to my height and looking into my eyes. I could tell he was going to beg for me to understand. I didn't care about anything he was going to say. I didn't even care about what would happen to the world at that moment. I only cared about seeing him one last time... before I knew, in my heart, that I had to let him go...

"Faith, look at me," he started, "it's okay to be scared and confused by all this. It really is. I was confused by all this when I first saw them. How can we reconcile the existence of these alien life forms with the world that we know? But think about it: Are those aliens really that much worse than the ones already living on Earth? I'm sure Levi has told you about how so many of us are not truly at home in the world. So many displaced from who they were meant to be; soldiers who are alienated to their own humanity in war after war, slaves and beggars who have become alienated to their own war-torn and colonized homelands, children with cancer who have become alienated to their own bodies when their lives should have been beginning."

Hugo pointed back towards the endless non-colorness and grabbed my shoulders. "If all truth is truth, then why keep any of it from us? When every species in the universe goes beyond existence, what will it matter why? They say they're keeping us safe from astronomical objects beyond our control, but the truth is that we're just lab rats in their twisted experiment for evolution." He took out the book of infinite pages again and held it up to my face. "Don't waste this precious gift, Faith. All the world's death and pain? *You and I* can put an end to all of that. How many families have died and how many more must suffer... so that *they* can continue to play God?"

My heart wavered between two choices, as if the fate of the whole world depended on *me* now. My whole life, I didn't trust in my own ability to pick right from wrong. I was scared of doing something that wasn't my place doing. I loved my brother, and I trusted in him completely. I trusted his beliefs and I trusted in his concern for the good of humanity. I would follow him anywhere, even to the end of time. He was my light. He *is* my light. And I would give anything in the world just for him to be with me again.

My love for him was my life... but now, I saw that his love for me wasn't his life. This place beyond time and space was his new life, and no matter how much I wanted to give myself over to him, I didn't want to force the whole world to come with us.

I love him... So I had to let him go...

Without touching the book, I took his hands and closed the covers shut. I saw the hope in his eyes fade to confused horror. With this, I saw the non-colorness all around us return to the black darkness of space, and the stars twinkled back into existence as the Truth's black circle shrunk away from us. Hugo backed away from me, shaking his head in utter disbelief at the path I had chosen for the world.

"Why, Faith?" he begged. "Why are you letting this happen? How could you do this to humanity? How could you do this to me? I thought you loved me."

"I do love you, Hugo," I said, "and that's why I can't take that book."

"If you love humanity," he said, "if you love this world, you would do *anything* to save it from itself..."

"If I save it from itself, it will never find itself..."

"So to all those starving families and dying children, you're saying 'suck it up and deal with it!?'" he screamed. "You *know* this is for the greater good! *This* is what's best for humanity!"

"If I take that knowledge from the aliens, humanity never becomes what it was meant to be, and it will destroy itself as it enters that darkness. It's a quick answer for a deep problem that should take a lot of careful time to solve; it's an answer that will create endless pain that is worse than hell. If I leave the knowledge, there will always be a chance that we do destroy ourselves... but there will always be a hope that we will build ourselves up to the destiny that we were made for!"

Hugo fell down to hug my legs, and he was crying so hard, I thought he was about to throw up. "Faith... Whatever happened to wanting to be with me in Heaven? We can be together again... only this time, the whole world can know what we both did for it."

I rested my hands on his shoulders as he kept crying into my lap. Tears sprung in my eyes, and even though my voice was breaking, I told him, "We both want to save the world... but we keep forgetting that we want it to find itself and change for the better... I'm sorry, but this is so much bigger than you, me, or even *them*... We have to keep fighting for a better tomorrow no matter how long it takes... We have to keep hoping for a future beyond the horizon..."

"That's just so senseless..."

"Hugo, please. Let me take this burden from you. You go back. Go become who you were meant to be."

"No... It's too late for me now, but not for you..."

"It's *never* too late!"

"If no one deserves this gift of enlightenment I bring, then there really is no meaning to my life; there's nothing left for me on this planet anymore... Not even you..."

Then, he was gone. He didn't even give me another look as left me behind to keep chasing the Truth. Not knowing what to do with myself now, I looked down at my hands and wept into them.

I'm sorry, mom. I tried.

CHAPTER 35
LEVI

When I first saw the tornado, the only sound I heard coming from it was a ghostly whooshing. Now that it was roving towards us, the screaming winds were as deafening as a jet turbine and as powerful as a nuclear shock wave. The rooftops of some of the observatory buildings were being peeled away and dragged into the wind, and trees swayed and twisted until their trunks were bent; I heard the sound of creaking and moaning in my surroundings until they gave way to a *crack* and tumbled away into the wind.

The fabric of reality seemed to be warping and twisting with the coming storm. I grit my teeth and let out a strained yell as I summoned up the will to keep standing against what I was beginning to believe was the full wrath of God. I tried to look back up... and I saw it.

It.

I wasn't even sure if you could call it an "it" since words cannot capture nor could eyes comprehend what was boiling in the heart of that tornado. The slanting rain and mist blasted against my face, almost completely blinding me. To stand against the storm, I grabbed onto one street sign and wooden post after another.

For a while there, I wasn't sure I was even going to make it there, but something in the air... I have no way of explaining it, but it felt as if something was somehow holding it back? The winds didn't die down, but as the leviathan came closer, the winds somehow didn't increase. When I did manage to reach the front door of the control room building, I forced the door open against the wind pressing down on me until I was able to slip through the door's slight aperture.

When I was finally inside the control room building, I rested my head against the door to catch my breath. To my disbelief, I heard what I thought was the raging wind outside dying away to silence. I looked out the window: It was still raining and the trees were still rustling, but the wind didn't look like it was strong enough to be tossing around heavy objects through the air. By then, I would have expected the tornado to have fallen upon the observatory and torn it to shreds.

A stillness had come into the air.

But then I saw the agents of the Blob fanning out around the building's perimeter, with Phoebe rushing down towards me. I remembered myself and pushed forward towards the control room; besides the flickering hum-buzz of the fluorescent lights and the echo of my rushing footsteps down the corridors, I didn't hear anything from any room. When I finally got to the control room, I rammed the door and scanned around looking for Faith.

"Faith?" I called. When there was no response, I called louder, "Faith, it's me, Levi. You can come out now." No response again. I took to looking under the desks and opening the doors to each of the closets. There were no visible holes in the roof or walls left by the tornado.

My searching eyes moved over the paper-covered floor and they found the onyx-black BCI, lying on one of its temples with one of its short-circuited lenses flickering white and purple. I picked it up and looked over its cracked lens, trying to come up with other possibilities as to what happened to her. When the BCI at the Museum of Science exploded, Hugo's body was still intact. My thoughts then wandered to two possibilities: She came out of it alive and left the building long before the storm reached her... or she somehow disappeared into thin air...

I saw something else flash in the lens of the BCI; the image of something I had hoped would have been long forgotten by now; a memory not long after Hugo passed from this world to the next. I saw hundreds of granite crosses under a gray sky. I saw a little girl dressed in black, placing a dandelion she plucked from the ground on the cross in front of her as her mother left her behind without so much as a look back.

The door behind me burst open, and before I could have gotten the chance to react, I felt myself get tackled to the ground by two of Phoebe's cronies. The BCI slipped from my hands and shards of glass burst from the goggles. When they were done searching my pockets and cuffing my wrists with a zip tie, they lifted me back up to my feet. The two gripped my shoulders and stood by as all three of us watched Phoebe pick up the shattered remains of the BCI; a failed relic of humanity's future. She picked it up and turned it over in her hand, looking more unsure of what to do with herself than with the goggles.

Still looking at the goggles, she asked, "Where is she, Levi?" When I didn't answer her, she shook her head annoyedly and told one of her cronies, "Roberto, you and your men search the area; she couldn't have gone far. Let's just hope that tornado didn't kill her."

"Where is Ms. Landing?" I finally said.

Phoebe shot me a glare, and she considered me with a bewildered regard. "You're not gonna ask how your brother's doing after that breakdown you just saw?"

"I know where my brother is," I said curtly before repeating, "and I'll check on him soon enough. But I need to know where you're keeping Ms. Landing *right now.*"

"Why?" she asked.

"Because I think I know where Faith is now."

"Where is she then?"

"No, you first."

Phoebe scoffed, "You know, you're really not in any position to make any demands, Levi."

"It's not me you're going to have to cooperate with," I answered. "It's Faith you'll have to take this up with."

The sneer disappeared from Phoebe's face, and I could tell that she was coming to the same conclusion I did. Still, she looked at me with a half-turned face and said, "You're covering for Faith, aren't you? You're buying her time by sending us on a wild goose chase so she can have more time to get away."

"That makes no sense."

"Bullshit."

"Where on Earth can she run off to!? Hugo's gone and you have her mom in—"

"But he isn't *really* gone, is he? Maybe she already has the information that he needed to tell her, and now, she's gone off to find another mainframe to upload it to. Another virus like the one yesterday, only this time, she'll follow through and take down the nation's grid."

"Just humor me for once, okay? If I'm wrong, I'm wrong, but you don't even have to send all your guys with me and Ms. Landing to find out for sure."

"Send you *where?*"

"Phoebe," I begged, "there's no reason for us to trust each other anymore, but you can trust that Faith's mother is the only person she has left in the world that she can trust."

"And why can't she just talk to you?"

"I don't know if she will even talk to *me* anymore after what we both made her go through, but if you ever want to see that proof, we have to try. I'll tell you where she might have gone. But I'm only going to ask one more time, otherwise, I'm only so happy to let Faith find her own way in the world: *Where. Is. Ms. Landing?*"

CHAPTER 36
LEVI

When I told Phoebe why I needed Ms. Landing to come with me to see if we could find Faith, I was hearing myself and even I thought I was sounding insane. But when I picked up that BCI, I saw something in the lenses: A place Faith and I frequented after Hugo's death. But there was something to the image that made me believe that I was seeing more than just a location; I saw a shadow of her soul that seemed beyond any consolation. I felt so helpless as to what I would have been able to do if I was able to find her again, and I realized that I didn't have the will to become the man I wished that my father was.

I was sitting across from Ms. Landing in the back of a moving van. Phoebe stayed behind at Haystack to keep searching for Faith there, but she had two soldiers escort us: One was driving and the other was sitting right next to me, looking between us to make sure we weren't quietly signaling to each other. He didn't have to worry about that; I found it difficult looking her in the eye, and when I did steal glances at her, she was leaning forward with her hands clasped in prayer and her eyes far away. Beyond the gentle rocking of the van's trundling wheels, a sheer silence hung over all three of us.

Enoch was in the passenger seat with the other soldier, telling him where to go next without needing a GPS to track our location. Phoebe said that he was of no use to the Blob anymore, and that all his life's work belongs to it now. Outrage was the first thing that came into my heart, but when Enoch pulled me into a bear hug, I saw in his eyes that he was just happy that we were back together again.

As happy as I was to be with him again, I was also relieved that he wasn't sitting in the back with us... because I didn't want to have Ms. Landing see our bond and remember the times her family was whole before all that's happened these past few months. She lost her husband, her son... and she was praying that she didn't lose her daughter too.

"We're here," the driver said. "St. Francis Cemetery in Newbridge, Massachusetts."

Ms. Landing did a double take. "Levi, why did they bring us to Hugo's grave?"

Enoch answered before I could: "Guys, I think I see her over there."

"Faith?" Ms. Landing asked. I could see the alarm coming to her face.

The soldier next to me stood up and unlocked the van's barn doors. I followed shortly after Ms. Landing as we stepped out and looked around at our surroundings: A rolling grassland surrounded by groves of pine trees... and covered with countless granite crosses.

When we walked around the van to look for Hugo's grave... we all stopped in our tracks when we caught sight of her.

Set against the rolling fog and the orange-red light of sunset on the horizon, we saw her silhouette kneeling before that cross she and I always came back to after school. Without another word, Ms. Landing rushed towards her; the soldiers were just about to follow after her when Enoch and I stopped them and reminded them of the terms we agreed with Phoebe. They relented, but drew their guns again should any of us decide to run away.

Enoch and I looked back at Ms. Landing who, oddly, didn't sink down to Faith's level to smother her with hugs and kisses as we expected her to; instead, we watched her kneel behind Faith, watching Hugo's cross headstone as they shared in the memories they cherished with him. Their hands moved over the grass, as if to feel for something they wish they could touch one last time.

"How do you think she got here so fast?" Enoch asked before venturing an impossible explanation. "You don't think she..."

"My question is why would she come *here* if she was already talking with Hugo?" I cut off.

Enoch offered, "Maybe it's just closure? To say goodbye to him one last time?"

"Meaning she doesn't intend on seeing him again anytime soon."

I saw Enoch piecing it all together in his mind as he looked back at the little girl reunited with her mother. "So... she said no to Hugo's gift. But still, how could she have gotten here so fast? Could it be that whatever Hugo showed her had some kind of effect on her anyways?"

I opened my mouth to shoot down the insane idea that she somehow gained superpowers from our little misadventure. But I took more time to ponder Enoch's question. No, it wasn't superpowers, but... it was something much, *much* more. Whatever she saw in the Black Hole disrupted space and time, and perhaps it was enough to reshape her entire will. A new knowledge on how to navigate through space-time; a super-sight into the fundamental properties of existence... and it was given to someone who knew only how to fixate on the lives of those closest to her.

I walked a bit closer to get a better look at Faith, and I could see the effect that that kind of life has had on her soul; she cared so much for others that she didn't value herself. I saw by the look on her face that she felt so violated and used, so drained and aimless from her own compassion to the point where she became numb to a world that only passed her by.

But she never stopped giving of herself to help those around her, as if the whole world depended on it. She never stopped fighting for my attention after Hugo died, she never stopped enduring her mother's grief when no one would comfort her own, and when the impossible happened, she couldn't bring herself to give up on Hugo... even if he really was too far gone. But in her heart, she was cornered with nowhere else to turn to and no one else to trust in.

Then her mother came back to her... to bring her back to the world that she first brought her into.

I saw Ms. Landing tenderly wrap her forearms around her little girl's collar and chest before resting her cheek on the top of her head and whispering something into her hair. Whatever Ms. Landing said to her... it was enough to petrify Faith, making her grit her teeth and tremble as a frightening new intensity swelled in her broken heart. Tears streamed down her cheeks from her harrowed eyes. For too long, she desperately searched for some escape from all the darkness that carved her out and left her empty and longing. And now, I could see that she was standing at the edge of her own strained mind, finally feeling the free will she never knew she had locked away inside of her.

After quietly wasting away for so long, having suffered all the hardships and wrongs done to her patiently, she finally felt a hope she thought was lost forever; a chance for all the unbearable pain and anguish to finally end. Now, she was finally set free and made whole by the realization that there was finally someone, *anyone* who understood her... someone who cared... she mattered to someone... she felt wanted... she didn't deserve any of what happened to her, and she was allowed to let go and be who she was created to be.

I soon realized that all the connections she had to the world, to her bones, her cells, her atoms... they all started with her brother and her mother, for they were closer to her than she was to herself. I know this... because all of my connections to the world start with her now. I know it was love, but that word "love" felt like such a pathetic shorthand for what was really in my heart. It didn't feel sentimental or vulnerable; it didn't feel like some series of chemical reactions and signals in my brain. It felt more like... a veil had been torn away, and I had found some kind of cosmic communion with some revealed truth *beyond* myself... like I finally found who I truly was in Faith.

This is the Truth; the first and the last that will be what it will be; the universe's hidden code; the only reality that has ever been; a thing hidden ever since the foundation of the world.

I realize now that the universe had no real reason to come into being; everything came from an unknowable nothingness that didn't need anything. Without some original cause, nothing would have happened and it would have kept not happening forever. Whether or not it was divinity, for the universe to have existed at all... *something* had to have been sacrificed by that original cause; a mysterious first essence that was poured out and given to us freely not because the origin needed it to exist, but simply because *we* needed it to exist; the flowing movement of the cosmos that acted uncannily like sacrificial love. Something was given out of nothing, from which there was nothing to give, but gave anyway.

We see no God because the universe is the most complete act of selflessness; a creative self-emptying so that the universe can become its truest self. The cosmos courses through me, and that selfless, self-emptying of the origin point still courses through the cosmos. Yes... I see it now! That innate affinity looks and acts more like gravity and magnetism than just some subjective gut feeling; not a happenstance result of our crude biochemistry, but some universal, metacosmic "through line" that was incarnated in our biochemistry as a sentiment.

A selfless, self-emptying movement that proceeds from the origin of the universe; the movement that stirs change in the spiraling night sky; the movement that propels light and attracts celestial bodies to each other across the universe; the movement that synthesized particles to create life on Earth... is the same movement that entangles emotional bonds between hearts. A state of "Be-ing" *in* Love... and reconciling all the world onto Love.

And if everything really was created through the Word, and the Word is God, and if we really were all made in His image...

Then Faith is my communion...

With a tear starting in my eye, I finally answered my brother, "She got here by letting herself be guided by something within all of us... that is greater than us."

It was then that, without warning, an arc-shaped piece of the sky moved in front of the sunset. Enoch and I fell back a step as we watched in astonishment the New Moon flaring the orange-red sunlight that framed Faith and Ms. Landing like a halo. When the moon finally eclipsed the sun, the blinding light from the rose-colored ring of fire made us turn away and cover our eyes with the crooks of our elbows. When we felt the light beginning to fade, we looked back at where Faith and Ms. Landing were kneeling... and saw that they had vanished.

It took a while for the realization to sink in, but the soldiers behind us eventually ran back to their van to radio Phoebe and the Blob about what impossibility they had just borne witness to. I knew they were going to take Enoch and I back for further questioning as to what happened, but I looked up at Enoch and saw that he was just as staggered and relieved as I was that wherever Faith and Ms. Landing went, they were beyond the Blob's reach now.

I did wonder where they had gone. I wondered if they were somewhere else on Earth now, away from the traps of our society. I wondered if they went somewhere beyond space-time... or if they had been transubstantiated, now fully immersed in the universe's Love. But wherever they were, I hoped that they were in a better place now.

I walked through the field of crosses and came before Hugo's grave, reading the epitaph on the cross headstone once more:

UNTIL WE FINALLY MEET
AT THE END OF ALL TIME

I looked down at the grass where Faith and Ms. Landing put their hands... and I saw that a yellow dandelion had grown there. I knelt down and caressed its petals, closing my eyes and letting myself feel the gentle twilight wind brush over my face. As my fingers moved over the dandelion, for a moment... I read in one mundane thing all the universe's sacrificial Love. Rivers don't drink their own water, trees don't eat their own fruits, and the sun doesn't shine on itself; all of these truths shaped a world that led to this one flower that was waiting billions of years for me to find it.

I then gazed heavenward and saw a shooting star stream across the night sky, leaving in its wake a flaring trail of green and purple light that looked like the northern lights. I let my mind wander the billions of stars of the Milky Way that came alive in the night sky; letting the twinkling starlight shower over me like raindrops; letting myself feel their gentle, luminous serenity; letting the waking universe discern itself through me... through others... through the nurturing Love that moved the stars and connected me to those who gave of themselves so that I might go on... and made present in me the melancholy and sufferings of those around the world who have yet to experience this truth.

I prayed to the silence, unsure if there might have been someone... *anyone* out there listening. And in such silence, I thought I could hear the faceless voice of one crying out in the wilderness. A light so blinding, I always mistook it for darkness. He was prophesying the secrets of God's Word into the universe.

Being.

Becoming.

Loving.

In it all... I have Faith...

AUTHOR'S NOTE

The premise of this story drew from a range of different sources, but at the heart of it was the "Transcension Hypothesis," a proposed answer to Fermi's Paradox that suggests that all civilizations exponentially accelerate their technological efficiencies by compressing the space, time, energy, and matter of their technology to femto-scale Black Hole-like dimensions, which will cause all civilizations to leave physical reality and merge together at the end of time. Such an idea was formulated by the global futurist and foresight consultant **John Smart** mainly through his essay "Evo Devo Universe? A Framework for Speculations on Cosmic Culture," published by NASA in the 2009 book *Cosmos and Culture: Cultural Evolution in a Cosmic Context.*

One of the central elements of Smart's hypothesis was drawn from the zoo hypothesis, which assumes that extraterrestrial life refrains from contacting Earth to avoid contaminating the natural course of evolution and development. What helped form the basis of this book's plot, however, was a quote from page 14 of Smart's 2012 essay "The Transcension Hypothesis" regarding the possibility that an advanced civilization might be covertly monitoring and protecting humanity from existential threats: "...the clandestine monitoring program, even if it were true, means little to us as a matter of science or practice, as to be morally defensible it must be undetectable, except perhaps in rare cases of failure (note: great science fiction plot here)."

In the event of such a failure, I asked myself what might happen and what secrets about the universe might they have learned. To begin, I drew from the 1998 essay written by Seth Lloyd and Daniel Abrams titled "Nonlinear quantum mechanics implies polynomial-time solution for NP-Complete and #P problems." Important to note is that Lloyd is also the author of a 2000 essay that Smart cited to argue that Black Holes are the ultimate computers in the universe: "Ultimate physical limits to computation." While NP-Completeness wasn't a part of Smart's initial argument for computational complexity, I found the idea of creating a purely speculative mathematical algorithm that would help expedite accelerating complexity to a Black Hole Singularity to be an excellent McGuffin to get a broader point across in a fictional story.

Admittedly, I am not a cosmologist or astronomer, but the prospect of intelligent life not only existing, but also attaining cosmologically transcendent capabilities posed some incredibly fascinating metaphysical implications (especially when viewed through the lens of Martin Heidegger's *Being and Time,* Arthur Schopenhauer's *The World as Will and Representation,* and Kevin Kelly's idea of the "Fifth and Sixth Discontinuity").

To my surprise, the speculations on humanity's direction formulated by Smart and other futurists and cosmologists like him draw extensively from the Jesuit theologian and paleontologist Pierre Teilhard de Chardin, specifically his writings on the "Omega Point" and the "noosphere," where all the world's human consciousnesses and relationships as well as the entire cosmos at large will collectivize and culminate in a kind of Eucharistic communion with the Logos (For Teilhard, the Logos is Jesus Christ; for Smart, it is some ultimate point of universal complexity).

If humanity is going in a particular direction with the way it is advancing its technological capabilities, what kind of attitude should we cultivate towards ourselves and our duty to the world around us? Before we can interact with beings from another world, how do we interact with the beings that inhabit *this* world?

Smart is optimistic that such civilizations would be benign even with their technological superiority because he regards moral progress to be a developmental inevitability. On page 49 in "Evo Devo Universe," he claims that morality is part of the universe's preconditions of cosmological development that seem to clear the way for the postbiological transition of intelligences, and that to continue to believe in an "Accidental Universe," while politically and scientifically conservative, is ultimately self-destructive to our evolution and development.

As I see it now, our human perception of existence is made up of endless cycles of desires and dissatisfactions feeding into a false sense of identity and our connection to this world; Smart provides that, right now, we are in what he refers to as "net-dehumanizing" first and second generations of technology that are only *temporary* (See the 2007 SIAI Interview he gave regarding the question of whether or not technologies could cause us to disengage with reality). I don't necessarily agree or disagree that these phases are temporary, but my concern is whether or not continuing down this path towards accelerating change would exacerbate those pernicious consumerist attitudes and desires that do distract from or water down our authentic experience of the world.

To account for this contagious cycle of desire in our technological progress, I have chosen to focus on the work of another fascinating generalist: The 1990 essay "Innovation and Repetition," written by the Christian anthropologist and polymath **René Girard**, which suggests that what drives meaningful innovation in every corporation and nation-state is the imitation of other innovations through competitive desires (I find that this pairs well with theologian David Bentley Hart's concerns about how a fast-paced consumerist capitalist culture leads to the manufacture of false desires).

On page 19 of his essay, Girard states, "The main prerequisite for real innovation is a minimal respect for the past, and a mastery of its achievements, ie. *mimesis*." I find that his claim on innovative processes has great consilience with Smart's cosmological framework of *autopoiesis,* where complex universal change is 95% future-oriented and 5% past-oriented (See his presentation "The Goodness of the Universe" given at the 2022 *Stepping into the Future* conference). If aliens do exist that are on the exact same trajectory towards Black Hole-like technological capabilities as humanity is, as Smart suggests, I wonder if they too are beset with the same exact Girardian pitfall of horizontally transmitted inauthentic desires.

And here is what fired me up to write this story.

There is both a disappointing lack of scholarship on any topic of the technological singularity analyzed through the lens of Mimetic Theory and a surprising lack of fictional depictions of the Transcension Hypothesis. I wondered, then, in what direction was I going to take this story? During my preliminary research for the first draft of this book, I fell down a rabbit hole of macroeconomics and cryptocurrency manias and I stumbled across the venture capitalist and *PayPal* co-founder and CEO **Peter Thiel**, who gave a number of talks at some annual "Singularity Summit" conferences dealing with how the technological singularity might affect financial markets. Out of curiosity, I looked into his background and, to my surprise, I saw that he was a former pupil of René Girard at Stanford University and co-founded the Singularity Summit in 2006, at which John Smart gave a lecture on STEM Compression (Then called MEST Compression).

Two quotes by Thiel stuck out to me that helped me understand how I was going to flush out my story's themes. In a lecture he gave at the Singularity Summit in 2009, in the context of investors trying to recover losses after the burst of the housing and credit bubbles in the stock market, he said, "The way you actually solve it is through real technology, real innovation... and I think where we find ourselves in the world in 2009 is in a world where the only way forward for the developed countries is through rapid innovation and progress in science. It has to be more rapid than it has been the last [20-40] years for us to meet the kinds of expectations that are built into the very fabric of our society."

That same year, in an interview with Daniel Lance, Thiel said in regards to Girard's philosophy, "I'm not always panglossian, optimistic, [but] I do think that any hopeful future of the 21st century is one where there will be more good mimesis than bad mimesis. The forms of transcendence people will be buying into will be healthy, not fake." Therein lies the consilience between the Transcension Hypothesis and Mimetic Theory: The acceleration of technological innovation being driven by built-in expectations in our society; expectations that can be reoriented towards a healthier disposition towards our connectedness to the world.

The escalating mimesis of a noosphere driving accelerating autopoiesis.

So what happens, then, when we, fraught as we are with mimetic consumerist attitudes, make contact with other intelligent life forms who have transcended prematurely before they themselves have even had a chance to reorient their own inauthentic desires? If they see time and space differently from inside the Black Hole, will our perception of a continuously linear space-time be so dramatically altered, that we will have to redefine what we understand as "the real?" If that's the case, will the false desires that give shape to our perception of reality commingle and compound with *theirs* until *our own sense of human identity* becomes unrecognizable?

As interesting as these questions are for fiction, I do want to make it especially clear that I have endeavored to adumbrate the aforementioned authors' ideas in my fictional work as best as I could, but ultimately, my book is a work of fiction, and therefore does not capture the full scope of their arguments nor does it entirely represent their worldviews. I do not wish to present myself as an authority on these subjects; only as an enthusiast, especially in regards to how the topics of Black Hole informatics, NP-Completeness, quantum computing, transhumanism, and extraterrestrial life might pertain to certain political and existential questions.

I have taken many creative liberties to suit the book's plot, especially with regards to my depictions of the alien life forms of the Transcension Hypothesis. I therefore encourage all readers of this book to verify each claim or depiction I have made with sources I have mentioned before fully accepting them as true or dismissing them as false.

As for the plot itself, the characters of Faith, Hugo, Levi, Enoch, Phoebe, Ms. Landing, and the Truth, as well as the town of Newbridge, Massachusetts, are all entirely my creation. The Blob is based on the real-world U.S. foreign policy entity of the same name, but my depiction of it as a cabal of undercover operatives is entirely fictitious. All four generations of the BCI and their CPUs as discussed are fictional, yet hypothetical depictions of our ongoing relationship to our ever-advancing technological capabilities per Smart's cosmology.

Important to note is that, in Smart's view, Black Hole transcension would likely occur 250-600 years after the technological singularity, and it will be at least another 60 years before general AIs show up. It is my personal belief that, unless we somehow manage to prove that P=NP sometime in the near future, we are not yet on the cusp of a new breakthrough. But one day, we will be and we will have to be ready for it.

ACKNOWLEDGMENTS

At the end of my 2023 debut novel *This Cup,* there is an excerpt from chapter 1 of the first draft of *Extraterrestrial.* There is a good reason why it, along with the original premise, isn't a part of this new story that I've chosen to tell. I want to thank **my parents** who, after reading the first draft, told me that they thought that the theme wasn't as actualized as it could have been. It was **my father** who encouraged me to relentlessly interrogate every principle of reality that I took for granted and to continuously strive for truth in whatever endeavor I chose to undertake; it was **my mother** who cultivated in me a fascination with the field of ontotheology that opened new avenues of inquiry for me in the fields of cosmology and metaphysics, and it was her who convinced me that the foundation of the entire universe is *kenosis.* I also want to thank **my brother Gabriel,** whose enthusiasm for technological innovation only compounded my fascination with humanity's next step in its evolution.

I am so very grateful to **John Smart** and his agent **Alvis Brigis,** both of whom took time out of their incredibly busy lives to sit with me and discuss possible points of dialogue between Girard's Mimetic Theory and Smart's Evo-Devo Theory. Both gave me some incredibly fascinating pointers and thought experiments to help me decide what direction I was going to take with this novel, especially in regards to the role of the "synaptic self" in the interdependent network collective mind as well as the overlapping dynamics between the cemi field theory and Black Hole physics. Once again, a big thanks to the lovely people at Cassidy Cataloguing Services, Inc., in particular **Paula Perry,** who greatly assisted in properly classifying my books.

I will also never stop being grateful to my mentor at Holy Cross, **Professor Mathew Schmalz,** who first introduced me to René Girard's thought in his Religion and Violence seminar and who continues to inspire me through his efforts to build bridges and open dialogues between Christians and other world religions. I will also never stop being grateful to my AP English Language and Composition teacher **Eamon Cunningham,** who not only gifted me a copy of Ray Kurzweil's 2005 book *The Singularity is Near,* but also fostered in me a love of literature and rhetoric.

I would also like to thank my cousins **Francisco** and **Faustino Santana.** Through all of our discussions and rather intense debates (to say *the absolute least*), I always came away with a new way of seeing and understanding how things work in the world. It was Francisco who strongly encouraged me to explore how the literal million-dollar question (per the Clay Mathematics Institute) of NP-Completeness might pertain to the Transcension Hypothesis. I would also like to thank my friends **Brendan Joseph-Torres, Gabriel Beltrane,** and **Nelson Rosa,** whose discussions of popular culture, metaphysics, and religion have greatly supplemented this creative endeavor.

Turn the page to read an excerpt from

THIS CUP

BY

PAUL FABIAN

CHAPTER 1

Glastonbury Tor
Somerset, England
September 14th, 1938

The pale white sunlight of dawn peaked over the clouds and kissed the patchwork of sheep pastures and enclosed bocages of England's Somerset Levels; verdant growths of rush and bracken were sparkling with the brisk morning's foggy dew; amid the lush tree lines, the sails of stone tower mills spun over boggy mires while shepherds herded their free-roaming droves of livestock down the drovers' byways along the Levels' hedgerows and split-rail fences for the seasonal transhumance.

For 19-year-old ingénue Psalmodie Vingt-Trois visiting from Paris, Glastonbury's bucolic landscape was a far cry from the skyline of London: A grimy crucible of commerce, finance, and industry, where smokestacks and derricks vied against steeples and clock towers for the soul of the metropolitan city.

Though London's atmosphere was always choked with smog the color of dirty cotton wool, Glastonbury's was humid and sweet with an emanating earthy scent.

Psalmodie lay on her back, lost in the shade inside the lone looming tower of the ancient Church of Saint Michael, which surmounted a cloud-cutting hillock and overlooked the slighted ruins of the enormous Benedictine Glastonbury Abbey. Resting on her abdomen was a wooden mazer filled with fresh water; the magical cup so valued and desperately sought out by the locals. In that moment, only two things mattered: Her own knightly conviction, and the cup in her hands, all brought together upon this legendary Isle of Avalon—the very resting place of King Arthur himself—, as the gods seemed to have quietly fated upon her.

To drink from it for a chance at eternal life, as her father had always told her.

All around her, a vast and blanketing oceanic cloud flooded through the landscape and swallowed the horizon. Psalmodie felt the cool air of this panoramic void sweep over her chapped lips and her fair, faintly freckled face. She closed her blue eyes and inhaled the placid solitude of the enchanted Isle deep into herself.

Psalmodie knew it was not always this peaceful. Even in Arthur's time, when the Roman Empire still ruled over the Britons, the pagan Celtic druids convoked festivals where large wickerwork idols were stuffed with humans and animals before being set ablaze, burning the sacrificial victims alive. Such legends, she recalled, were written by Roman chroniclers, perhaps with the aim to smear Celtic culture. Such a ritual was a far cry from the Celtic motif of the enchanted cauldron, capable of resurrecting dead warriors; one of many inspirations for the Holy Grail itself.

Death became life and became death and life again.

As she reflected on this eternal cycle of existence, an odd blend of dread and relief made its way into her heart when she heard the sound of footfalls crunching over saturated macadam; the sound called her eyes to the Gothic archway of the tower, and she saw that standing under it was her friend, an olive-skinned Afro-Arab woman. Psalmodie's shoulders softened once she recognized the concern and disappointment in her friend's face.

"*Comment ça va,* Shiloh?" Psalmodie said; her soft voice was a thick, but dainty Anglo-Aquitaine accent.

Psalmodie saw the dark blue kerchief loosely tied over Shiloh's tousled, blunt cut brown hair, with some small wisps curling from her brow and temples, framing the sensitive features of her gamine face. Her soulful eyes were hazel, but they glowed a limpid amber color in the white dawn sunlight. Psalmodie also noticed that Shiloh had been wearing her usual attire: Calf-high cuffed boots over loose green harem pants along with a quilted burnt sienna jerkin over a muslin-sleeved pullover undershirt. Shiloh never did fit in with the traditional Parisian decorum, but to Psalmodie's pity, no one ever seemed to have expected much from an outcast foreigner anyway.

"How's your spiritual retreat up in Whitby going for you?" Shiloh asked with a weary cadence. "It seems like you're a hair off course. Or was it that you got off at London before your train left for York?" She stepped closer into Psalmodie's view, forcing a wan smile before dropping it back to that same emotionally exhausted countenance... almost as if she wanted to hurt.

Shiloh's presence atop the hill obviously presaged what Psalmodie knew would have been a caravan of uniformed goons and suits making its way up the hill's concrete path to apprehend her. Psalmodie pushed herself to standing and rushed to the archway to scan the foot of the hill. Just as she expected, she saw the straggling procession rising from the cruel world that lay beneath the cloud. The West Mercia constabulary and the curators from the National Trust, all there for the medieval mazer she had stolen from the Powell Estate all the way back in Wales.

The *Cwpan Nanteos,* otherwise known as the Nanteos Cup.

"I can't sleep," Psalmodie said. She turned to face her friend, although she couldn't have brought herself to fully look at her. "I can't eat. I can't breathe. Everywhere I go, I can't stop seeing him."

"Your father?" Shiloh asked.

A silence befell them as they stole uneasy glances at each other. Psalmodie fixed her dark blonde hair behind her ear, though her plait had already been unfurled. Then her eyes finally met her friend's gaze. "So how did you know where to find me?"

Shiloh shrugged. "Well, I *am* your roommate, and you don't do a very good job keeping your bucket list from me; you've hardly been quiet about this place."

"I know," Psalmodie said with a resigned chuckle. Her smile was short-lived and her abashed regard towards Shiloh turned more curious. Though Shiloh had enough self-control for two, she wasn't quite as headstrong as Psalmodie. Even so, since the day they had met, Psalmodie knew that there was always something underlying Shiloh's reserved demeanor. "You know..." Psalmodie started, "I read somewhere that there actually used to be an ancient Roman temple in Londinium dedicated to the mystery cult of the Egyptian goddess of rebirth, Isis."

Shiloh nodded indifferently. "And you're mentioning this to me because...?"

Psalmodie ventured, "For all your talk of God and religion and all that other stuff, you've always seemed too awkward with everyone on campus, but I'm sure there's nothing you can say about yourself that will really surprise me. Why don't you just talk to me?"

"About what?"

"About your parents in Egypt or wherever you're from. About you. About *anything.*" Psalmodie saw her friend's face had again turned downcast and distant. Without another word, Shiloh held out her hand to receive the cup that Psalmodie had stolen. Instead, she noticed Psalmodie reaching for something in her pocket. With shaking fingers, she produced a ripped piece of paper. "My father sent me this," Psalmodie said, handing it to Shiloh.

The paper read:

OVXSVNRMVHGFMVILHVZOVKVVWZMHOZKRVIIV
LECHEMINESTUNEROSEALEPEEDANSLAPIERRE

Shiloh recognized it was a French-annotated Atbash telegram. An ancient Judaic substitution cipher made up of a reversely mapped alphabet that corresponded to their opposite letters; A is Z, B is Y, and so on.

Translated, it read, *Le chemin est une rose à l'épée dans la pierre.*

Shiloh's face shifted. "What is this?"

Psalmodie engaged her friend and read verbatim, "'The way is a rose to the sword in the stone.' He's definitely trying to tell me something about *this cup!*" Her wild eyes leveled on Shiloh's. "Shiloh, listen to me. This Nanteos Cup, it has to be the best candidate for the legendary relic."

"Psalmodie, how do you know it isn't just another hoax?" Shiloh asked.

"It's not a hoax!" Psalmodie protested. "It can't be! My father said so!"

"Maybe his message meant something else?"

"How? This civil parish lies along the same ley line as the city of Lancaster, whose medieval crest was a red Tudor rose! And if this place is indeed the Isle of Avalon, then this ought to have been where King Arthur forged his sword Excalib—" Psalmodie caught herself and shrank back from what she saw in Shiloh's eyes.

"Just give me the cup," Shiloh begged, "and let's just go home. I've already spoken to the Trust; I told them not to press any charges if they saw that the cup was safe."

Stroking the wych elm grain of the mazer one last time, Psalmodie sighed and surrendered it to her companion. It was in Shiloh's hand, but Psalmodie did not let go. The two locked eyes, and she read the same sadness in Shiloh's gaze. When Psalmodie saw this, her face fell small and she nodded subtly in defeat. Then, with her tongue in her cheek, Psalmodie deferred the barren relic to Shiloh. Psalmodie paused for thought, but then broke away and brushed past Shiloh's shoulder.

"Psalmodie?" Shiloh called, following shortly after her before stopping at the terrace outside the tower. Some uniforms received Psalmodie while two others leisurely converged on Shiloh to receive the priceless artifact.

"We thank you, Mademoiselle al-Ahad," one of the men said. "May we have the mazer now, please?"

Shiloh responded with a sigh, "So you will keep your word?"

He presented his outstretched hand and responded, "We'll place her under arrest in the meantime, but as we agreed, my dear, so long as there's no lasting damage to it, we will not pursue any charges or fines and no one else will ever have to know. In any case, however, I should be frank with you: I don't think your friend will be able to come back to our museum establishments for quite some time now, if ever."

Shiloh looked away and nodded at this. She looked down at the mazer and turned it over to make sure that there was no lasting damage to it. Once she handed it over to them, she saw the small Coptic cross tattoo on her right wrist: The seal of her echoing past.

"*A'udhu billahi,*" she whispered in Arabic.

The clouds parted, and she saw that the many market towns and hamlet settlements of King Arthur's fallen kingdom had come into striking relief.

THIS CUP